Playing with Matches

by
Lee Strauss

Lee Strauss

Playing with Matches
by Lee Strauss
Cover by Steven Novak Illustrations
Photo Credit: Bayerische Staatsbilbiothek München/Fotoarchiv
Hoffmann
Copyright © 2012 Lee Strauss
ISBN: 978-1-927547-44-1

Second Edition

NOTE FROM THE EDITOR: This new edition has several minor revisions, including name changes to three minor characters, in order to add clarity and authenticity to the timeline.

Dedication

To my parents, Gene and Lucille Franke,
and my parents- in-law, Herbert and Martha Strauss,
whose own stories are reflected within.

"Your child already belongs to us. What are you? You will pass on. Your descendants now stand in a new camp. In a short time they will know nothing else but this..."
- Adolf Hitler

Prologue

1945
JULY

T he pillar of smoke rising on the horizon could only mean one thing: a farm, which meant food.

Emil Radle limped across the sloping field that was brittle and dry from lack of rain and irrigation. He lost his footing twice, falling, grabbing at his leg, his mouth opening in a wide teeth-baring groan. The first time he beat the pain, pulling himself back onto his feet, hunger pushing him on. The second time he gave into the primal urge to scream and cry, until sleep threatened to take him again. The warm sun beat down, heavy, his mind lapsing into a drug-like state.

Somewhere in his subconscious, he knew he couldn't stay there; if he did he would die. He pulled himself up again, shaky and quivering. Finally, a house came into view. Out of breath, he slipped through the narrow opening of a stiff iron gate and knocked on the door.

It opened and a thin, elderly man with an unshaven face looked him up and down. "Not another one," he muttered.

"Please, do you have a piece of bread? Anything?"

The man frowned. "How old are you, boy?"

"Sixteen." Emil wondered what he must look like to the man. He hadn't bathed or had a change of clothes in weeks. He knew his hair was too long. He shifted his weight nervously, rubbing his bad knee.

The man noticed. "What's wrong with your leg?"

"Injured on the front."

The man sighed. "I don't have anything left. Someone knocks on my door every hour looking to eat."

As if on cue, Emil's stomach growled. "Please, I beg you. I'm starving."

The man's shoulders slumped. His face was drawn, fatigued, and his eyes were watery, as if he were about to cry.

"Wait here." He pointed to a rickety chair on the patio, and Emil let his weary body drop into it. The man returned with a coffee cup and handed it to Emil. "I have a cow out back. She doesn't give much. It's all I have."

Emil slurped it up. It was like a drop in a very large bucket, but it would keep him going for a while.

"Where are you headed?" the man said.

"Passau."

The man whistled. "That's a long way from here. At least two hundred kilometers."

"Yes," Emil said, handing the cup back. "But it's my home. I have to find my family."

"All the trains are out," the man said. "The roads are too damaged in most places for automobiles."

"I know. I'm walking."

"That will take you weeks." The man glanced at Emil's bad leg and sighed again. "At least you are young. I wish you the best."

"Thank you, sir."

The man offered his hand, pulling Emil to his feet. Emil said goodbye then turned to the road. *Step, limp, step, limp,* he headed south.

Behind him, Nuremberg lay in ruins, a beaten down giant.

Chapter One

1938

OCTOBER
Passau, Germany

H einz Schultz's word could send a man to prison. Though only a youth of fifteen, he was strong, tall, and blond. The boys in his *Deutsches Jungvolk* unit esteemed him and feared him.

And they wanted to be just like him.

Mesmerized, Emil sat straight and attentive. He didn't want to miss a thing Heinz might say or an opportunity to be noticed by him.

Heinz grabbed a pointing stick and tapped a well-worn map of Europe that was thumb-tacked to the wall. "This is a map of Europe from 1871."

He stopped abruptly in front of another, newer map. "And this is a map of Europe as she looks now. What is the striking difference?" His eyes scanned the room before landing on Emil. "Emil?"

Emil squeaked, "Germany is too small?"

"YES!" Heinz shouted. "Germany is too small. Much, much too small." He pointed again to the first map. "Here we were larger, though not yet great enough. And here," he swiveled back to the second map. "We are so tiny, you need a magnifying glass to see us. This is injustice!"

The severity of Heinz's convictions had grown since his voice had changed. It seemed to Emil that Heinz's voice came from his gut now rather than his head and he couldn't wait until his own voice finally changed. Not yet eleven, Emil knew he had a while to wait which frustrated him. It was hard to act tough when you sounded like a girl.

Heinz stood stiff, hands behind his back, studying each of his students until they were all white in the face with fear. He whispered, "Who is to blame?"

Friedrich slowly raised his long, skinny arm. Though the same age as the rest of the boys, he was much taller, with long, thin legs. He reminded Emil of an ostrich.

"The Jews," Friedrich answered.

Heinz's head bobbed in affirmation. "Correct. The Jews. And how do we know this?"

Friedrich continued, "They hurt the war effort by stirring up bad feelings against the government. We lost the Great War because people lost heart when they heard these lies."

"Jews and Communists," Heinz said. "They are the real enemies of Germany."

Emil tried to remember what his father had told him. Germany had lost the Great War because they thought they could win it quickly. They had underestimated their enemies. In the end, they hadn't enough soldiers left to finish the job.

But according to Heinz, his father was wrong. Germany's defeat was actually due to these other people, though, he still didn't fully understand what they did to cause their fall.

"We *were* a great nation," Heinz continued. "We *are* a great nation. And one day we *will be* an even greater nation."

Emil felt like a strong wind was pressing him against the wall.

After a long meaningful pause, Heinz said. "Give me examples of our superiority."

Emil's hand shot up, and then realizing he wasn't sure what answer Heinz wanted, quickly brought it down again. Heinz called on his own younger brother, Rolf.

"We are white, Aryan, and not Jewish."

Rolf said this like he was better than the rest of them, Emil thought, just because he was Heinz's brother.

Heinz nodded in agreement. "Others?"

Friedrich thrust his arm up again. "We are athletic and fit."

Moritz shifted uneasily in his chair; Emil knew his hefty friend wasn't exactly the most coordinated person. This time Emil raised his hand and left it up.

"Emil?"

"We are intelligent." All eyes were on him. Heinz waited. Why? Should he present an example? A model glider hung above the table prompting him. "We built the *Luftwaffe*."

"Indeed," said Heinz. "The mightiest air force in the world!"

"One day I will be a pilot in the *Luftwaffe!*" Emil boasted. The continued attention caused crimson flares to rush up his neck.

"A noble goal, Emil," Heinz said. Emil sat up even taller if that were possible.

Heinz then nodded to Johann who picked up his guitar and led the boys in a boisterous rendition of *Deutschland, Deutschland, uber alles*: Germany, Germany over all.

"Time's up," Heinz said after checking his watch. "But next meeting we have a surprise. There will be a test of courage. Bring swim wear."

Chapter Two

I t only took a flick of his wrist, a quick masterful nudge that propelled the beech wood piano lid in motion, dropping it shut.

The scream that ensued caused Mother to spring from her chair in the kitchen where she enjoyed her Saturday morning coffee, fresh cream no sugar.

"*Ach du Schreck!*" Mother said, her house shoes click-clacking across the wooden floor. "What happened?"

Helmut's small face erupted, fluid springing from his eyes and nose. He raised his purpling finger as evidence, wide sobs preventing him from creating words. With his other hand he pointed.

"Emil, what did you do this time?" Mother squatted low and wrapped Helmut's bruised finger in a tea towel. "Come to the kitchen, Helmut," she said. "Let's get some ice."

Fleetingly, Emil felt something similar to remorse. Still, it was the younger boy's fault. "He should've moved his hands. He saw me coming. He's so slow."

Helmut's eyes flashed angrily, and with small hiccups he defended himself. "I didn't see you, Emil, you idiot!"

Helmut's incessant, talent-less plunking had driven Emil mad, probably drove the whole neighborhood mad. He'd pointed this out earlier to his Father. It was *his* fault. If *he* had done something, Emil wouldn't have taken such drastic measures for peace and quiet.

Helmut continued to whimper, curled up on a chair with his left index finger wrapped in ice. He looked so small there and Emil fought an uncomfortable growing sense of regret. He pushed it aside.

Father entered the house at that moment, newspaper under one arm. He wore what he usually did on a Saturday, trousers and a white undershirt. "What's going on here?" he said, taking in the red face of his youngest son and the defiant look of his eldest.

Helmut, his lips still quivering said, "Emil, slammed the piano lid down on my finger."

"Father, he was making a racket. I couldn't stand it any longer. *You* should've stopped him."

Father and Emil locked glares. "Yes," Father said, slowly. "If anyone was to stop him, it should have been me. I am head of this house."

"Only under the *Fuehrer*."

Mother gasped. She braced herself against the counter before systematically depositing dirty dishes into the sink one by one.

Father dropped the newspaper on the table. "The *Fuehrer* doesn't yet live in this house with us, Emil."

"Mother," Emil said, avoiding his Father's last comment. "Where is my uniform?"

Mother's shoulders stiffened. She sighed, long and steady, a sound like air escaping a tire, and turned back to Emil. The skin around her dull grey eyes gathered at the corners. "You're not going to *Deutsches Jungvolk* again today, are you?" She wiped her reddened hands on her apron. "That's the third time this week."

"That's hardly too often. Heinz Schultz says we have much to learn and prepare for. Today there is a test of courage."

Mother's gaze landed on Father. Emil felt like they shared a secret language they spoke together with their eyes. "Peter?"

Father lifted his chin, darkened by yesterday's stubble. "Really, Emil? Don't you think it's a bit much? Family time is important, too."

Emil hated it when he sided with her. It was a weakness. Father had become weak. And Mother could be so suffocating.

"Heinz Schultz says all of Germany is our family now. What is best for the Fatherland must come first."

"But, we are still your blood family, Emil. Don't forget that." The muscle in Father's jaw twitched. He picked up his paper and settled on the sofa.

Mother let out another pointed sigh. "What do you do with so much time there, anyway?"

"Lots of stuff." Emil felt the tightening of short patience in his chest. "We sing and march, play sports, hike, read maps." Mother's weary expression didn't change. "And we learn about the greatness of Germany and our *Fuehrer*. It's fun. I don't see why you and Father are so concerned."

Helmut moaned and Mother rushed to his side. Anything to avoid his point, Emil thought.

"Come upstairs with Mama," she said.

Emil grimaced. Helmut was five years old, yet he still clung to Mother like a baby. Emil was in no real need of his mother anymore. He cleared his throat as they started up the stairs.

"Mother, my uniform?"

She paused, studying him through the railings. "It's hanging out on the line." Then as an afterthought, she added, "And, while you're out there, bring in the potatoes I dug up this morning and take them down to the cellar."

Outside, Emil unpinned his uniform–brown shirt, black pants–and stuffed them under his arm. Ignoring the basket of potatoes by the door, he went back into the house.

Father had the radio on: *"...unemployment in Germany is the lowest it has been in years, thanks to our good* Fuehrer. *The creation of the autobahn promises more jobs for more men, and we await the day when, as our great* Fuehrer *has promised, there is an automobile for every family..."*

"See?" Emil said, pointing at the radio. Why didn't they get it? Adolf Hitler was the hope of their great nation. If it weren't for him, they'd still be a people lining up in soup lines and oppressed by France and Britain. At least that's what Heinz had said.

Emil went to his room, put on his uniform, and expertly donned a thin black tie. He tightened his belt, taking a moment to run his finger over the embossed image on the rectangle buckle: an in-flight eagle with the swastika gripped firmly in its claws, the words *Blood and Honor* engraved above. The final touch was an armband, shiny and black with a striking swastika on it. Emil gazed in the mirror and admired himself. *Not bad*, he thought, grinning at his wiry image.

Father and Mother were still in the living room listening to the radio when he returned. They huddled near the device, practically shoulder to shoulder, concentrating on every word. Mother's face had paled to the same color of the putty on the walls, her mouth forming a small *O*. *"...the Jewish problem is being addressed..."*

"I'm going now."

They jerked upright.

"I told Moritz I would meet him at the Dome."

Father stood. "Son, you should stay home today."

"Heinz Schultz says we are sons of Germany first."

Emil couldn't help but notice Mother's stricken face. He almost felt sorry for her. "Really, you are worrying too much."

He forced a smile, grabbed his jacket and satchel, and left.

Chapter Three

Emil zipped up his newly issued *Deutsches Jungvolk* winter jacket, feeling handsome and confident. And warm. He could see his breath shoot out in little ghost-like puffs.

Across the narrow cobble-stone street, old Frau Fellner swept stubborn wet leaves off her step. She wore an ancient winter coat with a silk scarf on her head, and she ducked when Emil appeared, pretending not to see him.

Emil chose to overlook this slight and shouted heartily, *"Heil Hitler*, Frau Fellner," thrusting his right hand in salute. Frau Fellner examined his new jacket with her dark little eyes before responding quietly, *"Heil Hitler."* She didn't salute, but again, Emil overlooked it, for now, anyway. She was a sad old lady who'd lost both her husband and her son in the Great War, and besides, she'd been their neighbor for years.

With his satchel firmly over his shoulder, Emil straddled his bicycle and rode passed the flat-faced, stucco row-houses painted pastel shades of yellow, green and red that lined his street, and down narrow, bumpy cobblestone lanes to the park near Saint Stephen's cathedral. Passau was a small city located on the tip of a narrow peninsula hugged by two rivers that merged at the eastern peak: the Danube to the north and the Inn to the south. A third smaller river, the Ilz, flowed into the Danube nearby.

Emil slowed when a waft of sweet warm bread coming from Silbermann's Bakery met his nose. Though he had eaten breakfast, suddenly he felt hungry again.

Plus, there was Anne. She had been his friend since kindergarten. Anne Silbermann had cute little dimples and dark ringlets that fell around her sweet chubby cheeks. The teacher used to put their desks together so they could share word books when the supply was short.

He remembered how Anne would offer to share her pencils with him when he'd forgotten his at home and how sometimes that translated into sharing sweets during rest break.

When he'd gotten older he'd learned to dislike girls, like his friends Moritz and Johann had, and he stopped sharing desks, pencils or sweets with Anne. Now the only times he ever saw her was at the bakery.

Someone had written on the window, *Juden,* Jews, in case there was a person left in Passau who didn't know the Silbermann's were Jewish. Beside the word was a childish profile drawing of a man with an extraordinarily large nose. The message was clear: don't shop here.

This was *The Jewish Problem* that troubled his parents. Emil understood why it troubled them; his parents had several Jewish acquaintances. It was impossible not to, as

18

many of the stores in town were owned and run by Jews, and not shopping from them would be difficult.

Emil remembered how Heinz Schultz had blamed the Jews for all of Germany's problems. Perhaps he was right, but surely Anne Silbermann never did anything to hurt their country?

A strange sensation washed over Emil as he rode by. Suddenly he felt nervous for Anne. He wanted to see her again. Even though she was a Jew, he wanted to make sure she was okay. It was foolish, he knew, but he couldn't help himself. He turned the corner and stopped to check his watch. He still had time before he had to meet Moritz.

Emil reasoned that the scent of the fresh bread was too tempting to resist and the next non-Jewish bakery was too far out of the way and would make him late. Not shopping at the Silbermann Bakery would definitely be an inconvenience to those who lived in this neighborhood. Now his mother would have to walk to the other side of town to buy bread.

Emil glanced carefully in every direction before slipping inside the bakery. When he saw Anne he smiled. *"Grüss Gott."*

She had changed since he'd seen her last. Taller, slimmer, her dark curls pulled back in a long braid. But she still had the dimples.

"Grüss Gott, Emil," she said with clipped feigned politeness. She regarded Emil's *Deutsches Jungvolk* uniform and sharp new jacket with thinly veiled contempt.

She hated him. He could see it in her eyes. He was one of *them.*

Emil's smile fell into a stiff line. All business-like he said, *"Eine Semmel."* He couldn't let himself say please.

He watched as she selected a bun from the bin and put it into a bag. Instead of the small talk and friendly jokes they used to make when he'd come to the bakery for his mother, it was painfully silent.

"How are your father and mother?" he blurted.

She seemed stunned by his question; her eyes flickered with emotion. Was it fear? Emil wondered briefly if she'd answer.

"They're fine, thank you."

Anne placed the bun into a paper wrap and handed it to Emil, and he in turn presented payment.

A shadow from outside blocked the sunlight coming through the window. An SS officer stood outside and peered in. A little quiver shot up Emil's spine. He knew he shouldn't have entered the shop. What now? Emil turned back to Anne; she'd seen the officer, too.

Emil side stepped away from the window and stuffed the bun into his satchel.

"I have to go," he said.

The bell above the door rang before he'd made it outside. The officer eyed Emil and then Anne.

"Did you make a purchase here?" he said to Emil.

Emil trembled. If he admitted it, he'd be reprimanded for entering a shop that was clearly marked Jewish. If he lied, the officer may demand to see inside his satchel and he'd be caught.

The officer seemed to read the dilemma on his face. He faced Anne. "Give the boy his money back."

Anne opened the cash drawer and handed the coin over with a shaky hand. The officer in turn passed it to Emil. Emil accepted and waited for the officer to demand he returned the bun. Instead he opened the door and gave Emil a look that said, *get out.*

Forgetting about his bike, Emil ran up the hill to the park without looking back.

Chapter Four

oritz was there when Emil arrived. He stood near a bench facing the Cathedral, its three copper domes bluish with age, sparkling in the mid day sun. He had his hands shoved deep into his pants pockets, and a bag bulging under one arm. "I'm not a good swimmer," he said when he saw Emil. As if Emil didn't already know that. As if everyone didn't already know that.

"You can swim the length of the pool."

"Will that be good enough?"

Emil shrugged. "I hope so."

"To be honest," Moritz lowered his voice, "I'm kind of getting tired of the *Deutsches Jungvolk* meetings. All we do is run, march and hike until our legs drop off."

"What are you talking about?" Emil said. "Everyone goes to *Deutsches Jungvolk*. You can't quit!"

"Settle down, Emil." Moritz glanced around and Emil followed suit. No other *Deutsches Jungvolk* boys were nearby. Moritz clumsily kicked at a pile of brown leaves. "I'm just saying, that sometimes it's, you know, hard."

"It'll get better, Moritz. When we're fourteen we'll be in Hitler Youth. We'll get to shoot guns. It'll be fun." Emil joined in on the leaf kicking. "Eventually, I'll join the youth air force division. I'll learn all about aviation. I've heard we even build a one seat glider!"

The wind whistled through the bare branches stirring up mini tornados of dried leaves and debris.

"Johann and I will have to join the youth motor unit," Moritz said. "We'll be in the army one day."

"You still think we're going to war?"

Moritz fussed with the collar of his uniform. "Why else do you think they make us dress like soldiers?"

Johann was already at the public pool when they arrived. They were joined by another *Deutsches Jungvolk* unit, twenty boys in total lined up. Emil recognized most of them; they'd shared a bus to the Hitler Youth convention at Zeppelin Field in Nuremberg. Adolf Hitler himself had been there and had said these now famous words that resonated in every boy.

"*... der deutsche Junge der Zukunft muß schlank und rank sein, flink wie Windhunde, zäh wie Leder und hart wie Kruppstahl.*" The German boy of the future must be slim and slender, as fast as a greyhound, tough as leather and hard as Krupp steel.

Heinz shouted out the requirements for the test of courage. The boys were to dive head first off the five-meter high board. A collective gasp echoed through the room as the boys watched Heinz climb the long ladder to demonstrate. At the tip of the board, he transformed into something almost super-human. Graceful and strong, he performed a medal worthy dive. The boys broke into spontaneous applause at the beauty of it. Emil had heard that Heinz was training for the next Olympics and Emil had no doubt that Heinz would win gold.

Heinz instructed everyone to jump into the shallow end, and immediately out again. Emil figured that shivering as they waited was supposed to stir up their resolve to go ahead with the dive, but from the looks on all the boys' blue faces, quivering lips, and shaky knees, it wasn't working. Like the others, Emil wrapped his arms around himself in an effort to keep warm.

Emil watched the boys dive in, one after another. Or, more accurately, he watched them perform spectacular belly-flops.

Then it was Johann's turn. He glanced back at Emil as he climbed the ladder. Emil nodded slightly, encouraging him to keep going. Johann seemed to share Moritz's lack of enthusiasm for the new order, Emil thought. He wasn't sure what to make of his two best friends anymore. But once at the top Johann didn't slow down. He threw his body off the board, also with a great belly-flop entry.

Emil was next. Fighting back fear—fear of failure and fear of making a fool of himself—he mentally reviewed Heinz's diving demonstration, pushing himself to copy the image.

His entry into the water was smooth, and when he surfaced, Heinz applauded. Emil couldn't stop the smile that opened over his chattering teeth. Being publicly acknowledged by Heinz felt amazing.

Moritz took his turn. His legs trembled as he walked to the end of the board. Emil felt nervous for him. What if the fear of drowning overcame him and he refused to dive? Or the fear of heights? Forty eyeballs stared him down. Johann bobbed his head slightly, "You can do it," he whispered.

Moritz curled his toes over the edge. Emil held his breath. Moritz closed his eyes, bent over to touch his knees, paused and then let himself fall.

He came up gasping, and Emil could tell by the expression on his face that he was both terrified and elated by what he had done. Emil let out a breath of relief. Somehow Moritz managed to dog paddle to the edge of the pool.

The next fellow to go wasn't so lucky. Slender and pale with wide, red-rimmed eyes, Volker had fallen out of a fishing raft when he was younger. Only his father's quick reflexes had saved him from being pulled under by the strong current of the Danube River. Emil was surprised that he'd shown up at all, but there was a lot of pressure to attend *Deutsches Jungvolk* and Hitler Youth. Emil had heard that Volker's parents had recently become members of the Nazi party.

"I can't do it!" he shouted.

"You better do it!" Heinz shouted back, "Or you will be expelled!"

Go, go, Emil mentally urged him on.

Then the unthinkable happened. Volker pushed his way back down the ladder, past the line of boys. Heinz grabbed his arm before he could get away, and threw him into the pool.

Emil watched in horror as Volker struggled for his life. No one dared to rescue him. They just stared, unbelieving.

Might is Right, they were taught. Hitler and the Nazi regime had no room for weaklings or cowards. It was called Socio-Darwinism. *Survival of the fittest.*

Volker's skinny arms and legs flailed wildly, his face breaking the surface in full panic. He didn't cry out for help. In fact, it was eerily quiet. Just the soft splashing of water, and the quick breaths of nineteen, shivering boys. Emil wondered, *would Heinz really let him die?*

By some miracle, Volker floated to the edge of the pool and his hand gripped the side. He pulled his face out of the water and gulped air.

His face was blue, his eyes wide with terror. He'd almost drowned.

With everyone watching.

Chapter Five

The first day of November was All Saints Day. It was a Catholic religious holiday and since Bavaria was primarily a Catholic region, it was also a government holiday. That meant Father had the day off and everyone was generally in a very good mood.

Even though Emil's family wasn't Catholic they'd adopted the traditions of their good friends, the Schwarzes, next door. Mother said it was important to visit the family gravesites and November 1 was as good a time as any. The cemetery had row upon row of cement markers: some plain rounded blocks, others elaborate crosses. Dry leaves that reminded Emil of the withered hands of old men blew over the well-kept landscape.

Tradition dictated that they visit Mother's family first, then Father's.

"She was so good," Mother said as they stood in a row, casting four, elongated shadows over her mother's grave. Bettina Heinrich 1860 - 1912. A tear coursed down her face as one did every year. She was always vague when Emil asked about how Grandmother Heinrich had died. Something about a sickness only women get.

They moved on to Grandfather Heinrich, then to Grandfather Radle and lastly to Grandmother Radle. It was the same sequence every time and Emil suspected Mother's affection for each one went in that order, too.

The Schwarzes came for the mid-day meal.

"Come in, come in," Mother said with a broad smile. "Karl, don't you look handsome." Frau Schwarz had parted and slicked Karl's red hair over to one side; and the bright white of his scalp formed a straight line. Emil sympathized as Karl's face grew as red as his hair with embarrassment and Emil was certain Karl would've taken his two pudgy hands and scrubbed his head if he didn't fear a stern scolding. Helmut came to his rescue and the two of them skipped upstairs.

"Lena, your home looks beautiful!" Frau Schwarz said as she laid out the traditional All Saints Day *Striezel*, a sweet braided bread that was longer than her arm.

Herr Schwarz shook hands with Father. "*Grüss Gott*," he said. A perpetual smile plastered his puffy face. "And thank God for the Catholics!" His rounded belly shook as he laughed, like he was taking personal credit for the day off and found this humorous. His skin had a scarlet hue, similar to Karl's, with little tufts of red hair like a halo on his bald head.

The pork roasting in the oven heated the kitchen, and after awhile everyone had rosy cheeks. Mother had all her best dinnerware on the table and the dining room glowed in the light of two, tall candlesticks.

At noon the Catholic Church bells tolled and they all took their places around the table.

Father prayed and the Schwarzes finished by crossing themselves. Then everyone passed the food around: the sliced pork roast, tender and juicy, the bread dumplings, and sauerkraut.

Before long Father and Herr Schwarz were discussing what all Germans talked about lately—politics.

"The *Fuehrer* just wants what everyone wants, to re-unite Germans scattered after the Great War," Herr Schwarz was saying. "As you know, Austria never wanted to be a tiny country floundering on its own. Besides that, the majority of the people there are ethnic Germans, so it's economically feasible for *Anschluss*, for the two countries to form one great one."

"But, after battling against German dominance for four years," Father said, throwing his arm around for emphasis, "how can you expect the victors of the Great War to agree to any kind of expansion of Germany?"

"I don't expect them to. I just don't know if they can prevent it."

Father's forehead wrinkled like soft leather. "You mean another war?"

Emil knew his father had fought in the Great War for a short while near the end. The thought of him fighting in a second war caused his stomach to turn.

"Not another war," Herr Schwarz said quickly. "I'm just saying this is how the people are thinking. They don't like how the German minorities are being treated in other countries."

"Now, now, enough politics," Mother said, "This is a day to rest—we must talk of lighter things." She brought dessert to the table, delicious vanilla pudding. "Boys, please eat some more. There's plenty."

Emil tried to understand everything Father and Herr Schwarz meant, then he did as Mother suggested. He ate and ate and ate until his stomach bloated out like a harvest gourd.

Afterwards, Emil played Kick the Can with Helmut and Karl in the back yard and in the late afternoon, it was time for *Kaffee und Kuchen*, coffee and cake.

Mother and Frau Schwarz re-set the table; a large round chocolate torte and the braided sweet bread from Frau Schwarz were displayed on silver trays. Mother's favorite silver coffee pot, the one she got from Grandmother Heinrich, was in the center.

"Come everyone." She poured coffee into small cups and placing them on their saucers.

Emil didn't know how he could keep eating, but he managed to wolf down a piece of each type of cake and wash it down with milk. He plunked onto the living room sofa, and groaned quietly.

Father and Herr Schwarz sat there, too, drinking coffee and smoking cigarettes in front of the fireplace. Helmut and Karl had gone back outside and the women were in the kitchen. Emil didn't think Father realized he was in the room with them.

"I got a memo from head office yesterday," Father said in a near whisper. "A list of names. Jewish names."

"Oh?" said Herr Schwarz, leaning closer. "What does it mean?"

"I am required to let them go. They are no longer permitted to work at the factory."

"That's unbelievable. How many names?"

Father took a long drag on his cigarette, and watched the smoke plume lift to the ceiling. "Fifty-three."

"That many?"

"I don't want to do it."

"Then don't."

"If only it were so easy."

Emil muffled a moan and pondered their conversation. What should Father do? Emil personally had nothing against the Jews, especially ones like Anne and her family, but what if they were in some way hindering the growth of the new *Reich* like Heinz and his teacher, Herr Bauer, said? Emil only wanted what was best for Germany. He loved his country. *Was it possible Father didn't?* That idea sent a shot of fear through his bloated body. How could Father not love Germany? Everyone did. At least, everyone at school and *Deutsches Jungvolk* did. He wouldn't want Heinz to hear the way his father spoke sometimes.

Emil didn't understand everything that was going on around him, but there was one thing he was sure of. He was glad not to be a Jew.

Chapter Six

A week later, on his way home from school, Emil took a detour. He wouldn't admit it to anyone, but he was checking up on Anne. Why, he didn't know and he berated himself for being so stupid. If he were to follow the Nazi decrees, he would avoid everyone who was Jewish.

Truth was the Jews were in big trouble. Bigger trouble than ever before. Ernst Von Rath, a low-ranking Nazi stationed in Paris had been recently shot and lie on his death bed. The shooter was a Jew who apparently was protesting the poor treatment of his family in Poland. This "disgrace" had been a top news story on the government radio station and headlined on the national newspaper chains.

Icy air nipped at his ears. He rubbed them vigorously with chilled fingers, and then blew warm breath on his hands.

The crisp, dull grayness that filled the November air distracted him at first from the extra activity in the square. There were more police than usual, more soldiers and a rumble of heavy vehicles behind him caused Emil to spin around. A small troop of SS men followed the trucks. They marched in formation staring straight ahead with stern

31

expressions, like well-oiled machines. Emil spotted Herr Schwarz in the crowd that had gathered and ran to him.

"What is going on?" Emil asked.

"Von Rath died." Herr Schwarz's normal smile was knotted in a frown so tight; Emil thought his face would implode. "Just stay out of their way."

The trucks stopped suddenly and soldiers with sticks, and bats, crowbars and other types of archaic weapons in their hands, fanned throughout the market district.

Then Emil witnessed the first strike. He sprung back as shattered glass hit the street. The crowd, surprised by the unprovoked burst of violence, screamed and the shopkeepers, whose stores were being vandalized, ran outside yelling and shouting.

"Stop!" shrieked one merchant, only to have his cries answered with a severe blow to the head.

All around Emil and up every street, they smashed the windows; the shrill of glass breaking, sharp splinters, sparkling in the light, splayed on the street. The crowd thinned, some running for home, others looking for a safe place to watch the show.

Emil's legs felt frozen to the spot.

Were they crazy?

A shower of glass tinkled on the ground near him and he snapped to his senses ducking low behind a parked car.

A cacophony of voices shouted, "Stop! Please, stop!"

He recognized the men who protested, the shop owners being attacked. They were all Jews.

The soldiers threw out clothes, shoes, jewelry, food items—all the merchandise from the Jewish shops were flung into the streets.

Mayhem broke loose. People screamed and cursed, "Jewish Pigs!"

A flurry of glass. Emil ducked lower, covering his head.

Stunned, he witnessed people, non-Jews he'd known his whole life, scoop up these articles that didn't belong to them and scurry away.

The soldiers pushed the Jewish men who dared to challenge them to the ground, kicking them, and tossing them into the backs of army trucks.

A couple soldiers approached Anne's shop. They had short wooden planks in their hands, and they were laughing. Emil groaned and muttered, "Oh, no." One after the other, they smashed the windows, shouting obscenities.

They pulled Anne's father, Herr Silbermann, out of the bakery, and dragged him down the road. They threw him in the back of an army truck like a sack of garbage. Frau Silbermann and Anne ran behind, screaming. Emil wanted to chase after the truck, too. *No, no! Stop!* Herr Schwarz seemed to read his mind, and grabbed his shoulder with his meaty hand, shaking his head. If he ran after Anne's father, he'd no doubt the soldiers wouldn't think twice about swinging him into the back of the truck to share the man's fate.

Anne crumbled to the ground; her mother fell alongside her, wailing. Emil wanted to go to them, to help them somehow, but he knew he couldn't. He just stood there, trembling.

Someone shouted, "Fire!" Plumes of smoke and flames poured from the synagogue. Emil couldn't stop himself from running down the block to stare. An SS soldier climbed to the roof and waved parts of the Torah, the sacred Jewish religious scrolls.

"We'll use it for toilet paper!"

These were Emil's Nazi superiors, his mentors, yet he was mortified. His mouth felt dry and thick, it was difficult to swallow. They expected Emil to cheer and celebrate what he was witnessing, but instead he felt weak and winded.

Emil's *Deutsches Jungvolk* comrades, Friedrich and Wolfgang, seem to appear from nowhere. They threw stones at the Jews as the SS dragged them down the street.

Friedrich saw Emil and waved for him to join them, his eyes popping with excitement, a crooked grin on his face.

"Com'on, Emil!"

Emil hesitated.

"Emil!"

Emil took a step forward, but he felt sick. He knew he should join them, show a united front, but he just couldn't. He pretended to twist his ankle and hopped around, moaning.

"Man, Emil," Friedrich spun towards him. "You're missing all the fun!"

"Sorry, I can't." Emil limped some more. Friedrich shrugged and ran off to catch up to Wolfgang without him.

Emil wanted to serve his nation and make her great again. He wanted to be a good Nazi, he really did, but when he thought of Anne and the terrified expression on her face, he shook his head.

He faked a limp all the way home.

Chapter Seven

Rolf knocked on Emil's front door early the next morning.

"All the *Deutsches Jungvolk* and Hitler Youth are required for street clean up. Heinz wants us to meet him in fifteen minutes."

Johann and Moritz were already there, brooms in hand, when Emil arrived. The older boys nailed plywood across broken windows; some cleaned up the synagogue.

"See what you missed," Emil said, gesturing to the streets full of glass. Johann and Moritz lived on farms further out of town and didn't hear about the assault until it was over.

Emil's breath hit the winter air like bursts of steam. Snow couldn't be too far behind. They were smart enough to wear gloves.

"I hear every town and city in Germany had *Reichskristallnacht*," said Johann. "The reports say the fanatical hatred of the Jews by the German citizens was stirred up by the slaying of Von Rath."

Emil frowned. From what he saw, it was the soldiers not the citizens that attacked the store shops.

"The citizens are exceptionally well organized for such a spontaneous event," Moritz muttered while scooping up a dustpan of glass, letting it slide into a bin.

The streets were too quiet. Normally, the shopkeepers would step outside their doors with friendly smiles, greeting potential customers. Today they were like shadows as they cleaned up their shop fronts with heads bowed.

It was like a ghost town, Emil thought. No one was shopping. It was eerie.

"What happened, Emil?" said Johann, shaking his head. "This is a big mess."

"It was loud. People were screaming. Glass shards fell from the sky."

Moritz poured another dustpan full of trash in the bin. He said softly, "They really have it out for the Jews."

Emil stomach churned with confusion. "The Jew *did* kill Von Rath. It's natural to be angry over it." Emil was angry. None of this would've happened, if the Jew would've just left things alone.

Would it?

Friedrich's sudden shouting echoed through the streets. "Yahoo! We showed those filthy Jews a thing or two, didn't we?!"

The boys put their heads down and continued sweeping. *Sweep, sweep, sweep.*

Across the street, Herr Jäger, a short plump man with leathery skin, stepped out of his shoe repair store and turned the key to lock the door. He had a spring in his step and was whistling. Emil was certain that the upcoming lunch Frau Jäger had prepared wasn't the reason for his joyfulness this time. He could see Herr Finkleman's new arm band. Red with a deep-black swastika.

There had been whispers that someone would be appointed to watch over their neighborhood, to watch everyone, to make sure they were in compliance with all the new laws. He didn't believe the rumors at first. But,

Emil knew at that moment that they were true. Herr Jäger was their new watchman.

Rolf instructed them to go home for the mid day meal, and to return in one hour. Before too long, Passau would be up and running like nothing had happened. Like *Kristallnacht* hadn't happened at all.

Emil was nervous about going home. Last night Mother had been in hysterics. She wept and prayed and mourned. The things she said about the Reich couldn't be repeated and Emil just hoped their shared walls were sound proof.

The table was in order and Father called everyone to it. He bowed his head to pray and at the end they agreed together, *Amen.* Mother passed the bread and the cabbage rolls around. They ate in silence.

The quiet was too much for Emil. "It's almost cleaned up," he said. "Things should be back to normal soon."

"Nothing will ever be normal again, Emil," Mother said, stiffly. "Not if the Jews are not welcome in our country."

Just then they heard a commotion coming from the street. Emil beat his father to the front door.

A woman yelled, "Let me go!" while two SS officers in black suits pushed her into a car. Emil recognized her as Fraulein Kreutz, a second grade teacher at his school. She lived in a flat two doors down across the street.

"What's going on, Father?"

He shook his head. Herr and Frau Schwarz from next door watched, too.

"What on earth could Fraulein Kreutz have done?" Frau Schwarz said.

She must've done something awful, Emil thought. *Something harmful to the Reich.*

There were no formal announcements at school the next day, but Emil heard the students talking in the hall. Fraulein

Kreutz had criticized the swastika. Herr Jäger had overheard and reported her to the police.

Herr Bauer acted like nothing out of the ordinary had happened. He told the class to stand and recite the refrain he had written on the blackboard.

Your name, my Fuehrer, *is the happiness of youth; your name, my Fuehrer, is for us everlasting life.*

He made them say it three times.

Chapter Eight

"Life is a struggle," began Herr Bauer. He taught math and literature but seemed to have a special interest in racial science.

"It is a struggle for survival. He who wants to live should fight. He who doesn't want to battle in this world of eternal struggle does not deserve to be alive. Therefore it is the utmost of importance to be strong."

Herr Bauer paced across the front of the class, hand on his chin, finger to his long nose. The back of his rounded, bald head thickened at his neck, reminding Emil of a gigantic thumb.

"Just as plants and animals are divided into species, humans are divided into races." He stepped up to the blackboard, picked up a piece of chalk and wrote: *Culture Founders*.

"Now, our very intelligent National Socialist researchers have gone back through history, studying all the advances in civilization and have tested the heredity of various historical societies and figures. What they discovered was that all important accomplishments in art, science and technology have been made by the Nordic or Aryan race. Therefore, this is clearly the only race of culture founders."

Emil, who sat in the desk behind Johann, saw his friend's shoulders slump as he dared to stare out the window. Emil poked him with a pencil while Herr Bauer scribbled *Aryan* under the words *Culture Founders*.

"Now, most Aryan people are tall, slender, have a small face and high-set, narrow nose, rosy-white skin, smooth, golden-blond hair and blue eyes."

Emil heard a little giggle come from Irmgard Schultz. She was Heinz's sister, and therefore, Emil thought, worthy of attention. Anyone studying the various characteristics in the room could see why she smiled and giggled. She and Rolf, who was her twin, were the only ones in the room who completely fit that description. Emil though tall, had dark hair. Moritz was short and stocky. Of the three friends, Johann came closest, though no one would call his nose small and he had brown eyes.

"Aryans are uncommonly gifted mentally. Therefore, they are outstanding for truthfulness and energy. Nordic men possess, even in regard to themselves, a great power of judgment…"

Herr Bauer paused and Emil thought his teacher was imagining himself to be the epitome of the Nordic male.

Herr Bauer continued, "They are persistent and stick to a purpose when once they have set themselves to it. Their energy is displayed not only in warfare but also in technology and in scientific research. They, *we*, are predisposed to leadership by nature."

He took a moment to scan his students' faces. Emil squirmed slightly when Herr Bauer got to him.

"Children, you are members of the fittest race and citizens of the greatest country on earth. Therefore…"

He grinned, strolling casually across the front of the class room. "… it is of the utmost importance that you remain racially pure. Under no circumstances should there be mating with people from a lesser race."

A round of muffled giggles circled the room. Emil felt his face grow red and saw that he wasn't alone. Johann's face was an unattractive shade of scarlet, too.

Herr Bauer returned to the blackboard and wrote: *Culture Destroyers*.

"Now class, who would be the culture destroyers?"

A flurry of arms waved in the air. Friedrich, Wolfgang and Rolf all had their right arms stiff, pointed towards the ceiling, faces bright and eager as if competing with each other over who had the longest arms.

"Rolf?"

"The Jews, sir," he said with a winner's confidence.

"Yes, you are right, Rolf, the Jews." Herr Bauer scratched 'THE JEWS' in big bold letters under the words 'Culture Destroyers.'

"These culture destroyers are tricky, clever and evil," Herr Bauer continued. "They want to rule the world, disguising themselves as one of us in order to destroy the Aryan race."

He paused, finger to nose, facing the class. "We know this is true by the fact that the Jews ran so many successful businesses. It is obvious that they cannot, under any circumstances, be trusted, and therefore, *Krystallnacht* is justified."

Krystallnacht *is justified because the Jews were good businessmen?* Emil didn't get the connection, but there was no way he dared to question Herr Bauer about it and be made a fool of in front of the whole class.

"Evidence to the superiority of the Aryan race can be seen throughout history," Herr Bauer continued. "Even literature, such as the common fairy tale points to the

41

prominence of the German race. Can anyone give me an example?"

Irmgard raised her hand. "Cinderella?"

"Yes, Cinderella is a great example." Herr Bauer propped himself on the edge of his desk. "Cinderella, our heroine, is obviously a racially pure maiden. All the pictures show her as blond, with blue eyes and physically healthy. In contrast to her is the evil stepmother, who is from some alien country, possibly a Jew. It seemed that Cinderella's father was a man of weakness, and thus his apparent lack of presence in the story.

"Our prince, also from a superior blood line, rescues Cinderella from her dismal situation. Clearly, a hero and brave warrior like those found in our own great army."

Elsbeth Ehrmann raised her hand, "Our great *Fuehrer* is my prince," she gushed.

"And mine!" added Irmgard and the rest of the girls joined in giggling.

Those silly girls and their giggling. Emil felt itchy with irritation and wished Herr Bauer would do something to shut them up.

Later that evening, Emil and Helmut did homework at the kitchen table. Father read the newspaper by the fireplace and Mother was next door visiting Frau Schwarz. It was quiet except for the sound of the wind whistling through the window and the rustling of paper as Father turned the pages.

"Emil can you help me?" Helmut said. "I don't get this."

"What?"

"This math. It's stupid."

Emil craned his neck over Helmut's work. Simple addition. He reached for Helmut's pencil, but before he could show him what to do, the slamming of the back door interrupted him.

Mother stood there in a daze. Her pale face blanched even whiter if that were possible.

She rushed to Father's side and bent down to whisper something in his ear. His eyes narrowed, deep wrinkles fanning from the corners.

"What happened?" Emil asked.

They both turned to face him slowly. Mother looked at Emil as if he had a gun pointed at her.

"Mother?" Helmut said in a small voice.

What was the matter with them? Why wouldn't they talk?

"Mother? Father? What's wrong?" Emil said.

Father cleared his throat. Mother shot him a look. "It's all right, dear," he said. "Emil, your classmate, Elsbeth Ehrmann..."

"Yes, Father?" Did she get sick? Die? Why would his parents care? It's not like they knew her.

"She reported her parents to the Gestapo. Apparently they didn't approve of the *Fuehrer*. Herr and Frau Ehrmann have been arrested."

"Oh." Now Emil understood. He'd never forget how his parents looked at him that day.

They didn't trust him.

Chapter Nine

1939
MARCH

As usual, Moritz, Johann and Emil cut through the park at St. Stephen's Cathedral on their way to *Deutsches Jungvolk*.

Emil spotted Irmgard and Elsbeth dressed in their League uniforms– narrow, dark calf-length skirts, white ankle socks with black flat-heeled shoes and white blouses with dark ties. They were laughing at something. Those two were always laughing. Irmgard tilted her head back to catch a snowflake with her tongue, her long yellow braids hanging down her back.

"I heard Friedrich and Wolfgang talking about them," Emil said, pointing. "They think that Elsbeth and Irmgard are pretty."

"Pretty?" Johann said, studying them.

"That's what I heard them say."

"I'm sick of hearing about Elsbeth," said Moritz. "We should all be so happy to send our parents to prison."

"Moritz!"

He glanced around. "No one heard me."

Elsbeth and her little sister lived with her *Onkel* and *Tante* now. They were members of *the party*.

"I suppose they are kind of pretty," Johann said.

"I guess," Emil said. The girls stopped, like they knew they were being watched. They giggled some more and headed towards the boys.

"What are they doing?" said Moritz, narrowing his eyes. Johann and Emil just shrugged.

"Good day, boys." Irmgard tilted her head and smiled. "Isn't it great? Don't you just love the snow?"

Jaws slacking, Moritz, Johann and Emil were too shocked by the fact that Irmgard Schultz was taking time to talk to them to respond.

"Cat got your tongue? You boys are nothing like my brothers, all they do is talk. About the Fuehrer, of course, so it's good talk."

The boys also didn't have much experience talking to girls. They cast worried glances at each other, egging each one on with their eyes to say something.

"I think they're shy," said Elsbeth. "Maybe we should meet later, show them how friendly we are."

Johann said quickly, "Uh, we're busy. Later."

"Maybe another time." Elsbeth wiggled her fingers. "Until then."

Irmgard waved and giggled.

When they were out of earshot, Moritz grabbed Emil's arm. "Don't ever do that again."

"Do what? I didn't call them over."

"But you thought about them, pointed at them."

"So?"

"So, I don't talk to girls."

"I do," said Johann. "My sister's a girl and I talk to her all the time."

"That doesn't count, you know what I mean. Girls are dumb. Not your sister, Johann, just other girls." He nodded his head toward Irmgard and Elsbeth. "Like those girls."

"All right, I'm sorry," Emil said. "Let's get going before we're late."

Herr Giesler could have been a movie star. He had perfect Aryan features, blue eyes, a wide, bright smile and a confident bounce to his step. He taught French and geography, and one day he showed up at school wearing his Nazi party uniform.

The girls giggled and sighed. Irmgard whispered to Elsbeth, "He's so handsome!" but everyone heard it. And everyone would agree.

After a chorus of "*Heil Hitler*," Herr Giesler excitedly unfolded a map and hung it on the board.

"Class, our new Germany!" he said. They all leaned forward as Herr Giesler pointed with a long stick to the boundary lines.

"First the triumphant *Anschluss* with Austria and now Czechoslovakia, including the piece that had been part of Germany before the Great War!" His eyes sparkled. "Our great *Fuehrer* has succeeded in getting back what was ours and more. Now we can breathe. Now we have *Lebensraum*!" Room for the people.

Moritz raised his hand.

"Moritz?"

"Do we have enough?"

"Enough what?" Herr Giesler asked.

"*Lebensraum*?"

That stopped him momentarily, but his bouncy energy immediately returned.

"Well, let's see. What do you think class? Do we have enough *Lebensraum* for our great nation? Do we need more?"

A rousing cheer erupted, "Yes! Yes! We need more!"

"There's your answer, Emil. Now for French. More good news! No more French. We will study Latin."

Wolfgang raised his hand. "Why are we no longer studying French?"

"Because French and other languages like English are languages for those who lack full intelligence. The French and the British, they can *not* be trusted. We are not in need of them and do not need their languages."

"What about the Americans?" Emil asked. "They also speak English."

"What do we have in common with a nation that loves Negroes?"

"Nothing?"

"That's right," Herr Giesler said, brushing his hands together as if getting rid of dust. "Nothing."

Chapter Ten

SEPTEMBER

"I bought the last of the rye bread at the bakery this morning," Mother said as she placed the basket on the table. "It's seems all the stores are running short of supplies these days. I bought two sticks of butter this time, just in case."

Emil joined his family for their morning meal. Outside the clouds blocked the rising sun, casting a cool grey light across the room and marking the end of summer. Father turned the radio on and hummed with the latest Marlene Dietrich song.

He spread butter on his slice of rye bread, placing a thin slice of cheese on top. His mouth was full when the music ended and an agitated voice broke through the radio waves.

"In the early morning hours a group of Polish soldiers crossed the Polish-German border and attacked the studio building of the broadcasting station in Gleiwitz..."

Emil's father threw his knife down on the table, startling both Helmut and Emil. "We're supposed to believe that!"

Emil swallowed his mouthful. "What does it mean, Father?"

"It means Hitler is going to get what he wanted all along. Now he has an excuse for war."

"Oh, no," Mother said pinching her eyes tight.

So, Moritz was right, Emil thought. They were being trained for battle. But still, something in him wanted to defend their nation and their *Fuehrer*. Why were they assuming the radio announcer wasn't speaking the truth?

"It must be necessary," Emil said. "You know how the Poles have been mistreating our people there."

"I know no such thing!" Father snapped.

"But the newspapers..."

"Don't believe everything you read and hear."

"What about Danzig?" Emil referred to the port city on the Eastern Sea that had once belonged to Germany. It was a major import and export city and lay in the narrow corridor of land in Poland that separated Germany from German East Prussia. Its inhabitants were mostly Germans. It made sense to Emil that at least that city should be returned.

"Besides, Hitler wouldn't lead our nation to war if it wasn't in our best interest," Emil insisted. "He wants a Glorious Greater Germany for us all!"

"Emil," Mother said, "war means one thing: death. Young men who should be living and dreaming about their futures will die instead." She threw her arms into the air. "God help us."

"Father, it doesn't really mean war, does it?" Emil said, ignoring her. "We've taken Austria and Czechoslovakia and nobody's cared. If they didn't do anything then, they probably won't do anything now."

Father shook his head and sunk deeper into his chair. Helmut climbed onto his lap, whimpering.

49

"Son, the world won't watch forever. England promised to defend Poland. If they don't, Hitler will not stop at invading them one day as well."

"Invade England?"

He wondered what this would mean, if war with Poland would really affect their lives in any practical way. Would they really go to war? He couldn't imagine it.

They left the table, and rushed upstairs to get ready for the day: Emil and Helmut for school, Father for his job as an office administrator at the clothing factory.

Emil passed Helmut, taking the steps two at a time, giving him a good nudge as he went by.

"Hey!" Then sensing their father coming up behind them, he whined. "Father, Emil pushed me."

"Emil," was all he said. That's when Emil noticed the dark circles around Father's eyes. His father hadn't been sleeping well.

Emil brushed his teeth and hair. His parent's bedroom door was cracked open and he could hear their worried voices. He pressed himself up against the wall of the hallway and peeked in. Father was dressed in a nice suit. That was the good thing about his job; the whole family always dressed respectably with quality clothes well ironed by Mother.

"I had to let all the Jews go. These are people I respect; they were hard workers and some of them I counted as friends. I could barely look them in the eyes; I was so ashamed. Now with this shortage of workers, it's very difficult to keep up with the orders." He shook his head. "And, Leni, they want me to join the party. If I refuse, I may lose my job."

"Oh, Peter. This is terrible." Mother was trembling. Father straightened his tie. Emil sneaked back to his room and waited for Father to leave. When he walked by their room again, Mother was kneeling by the side of the bed, praying.

Two days later, Herr Bauer made a big announcement.

"Britain has declared war on Germany!"

Gasps filled the air of their small class room, and Emil's stomach sank. His father and mother had been right.

"What does this mean for Germany?" Friedrich asked.

"It means that Britain will get what she deserves." Herr Bauer touched his nose then thrust his arm up high. "We will show her and the whole world how magnificent Germany is. We will triumph!"

Before the day ended France, India, Australia and New Zealand had joined Britain.

Emil bit his bottom lip nervously. War wouldn't come to their small corner of Germany, would it? Passau was as far away from Britain as you could get. Surely he and his family would be safe?

Chapter Eleven

1940
FEBRUARY

Anyone who owned an automobile had to turn it over to the state. All gasoline was reserved for the war effort now.

This created a situation not yet faced by the citizens of Germany. No vehicles to remove the snow or men to operate them, which resulted in snow piling up in the streets and walkways. The Nazis had a solution for this problem. Send out the women and give them shovels. Or more precisely, the Jewish women.

Emil had worked hard at not thinking about the horrible things that had happened to Anne and her family since the night of the broken glass, and so to come across her so abruptly one day was a shock. She and her mother were out in the cold, wearing only dresses with stockings and thin coats, shoveling snow off the walk a block away from the bakery they used to own. Their hands were bare and cherry red; their knuckles and tips of their fingers where swollen and blackish. Frostbite.

An officer stood guard nearby and showed them no pity. He saw Emil stop and stare, and with a subtle nod of his head, warned him to keep going. Anne saw him, too, and Emil quickly averted his eyes which started to pinch and sting. Walking away, Emil was overcome with emotion. Anger mostly. And confusion. Why should he care about Anne and her mother, they were just Jews.

But he did care. Anne had been his friend once. He had to do something, but what?

Emil's hands were warm, he had gloves. And he had an idea. Just before Emil entered the bakery, which was now run by a new non-Jewish family, he bent down and untied one boot.

Moments later he returned to the street with a warm sweet pastry in his gloved hand. He carried it down the street and when he came to the officer watching Anne and her mother he stopped. Out of the corner of his eye he could see them; shivering, cold, sunken eyes staring at his strudel.

Emil chatted with the guard.

"*Heil Hitler!*" he said.

"*Heil Hitler!*" The guard responded his eyes darting to Emil's pastry.

Emil took a bite. "Um, it's delicious. Warm. Sugar and cinnamon. There's only a couple left."

The guard understood the food shortage.

"Only a couple?"

"Yes," Emil took another small bite. "It's so good. Well, *Heil Hitler.*" He turned away and before long the officer left, no doubt headed for the bakery, Emil thought.

He had only a short time to do what he planned to do next. He caught Anne's gaze.

"Oh, my boot is untied." *Watch me*, his eyes said. He bent over, putting the pastry and his gloves on the snow, and quickly tied his boot. When he stood up, he marched away. Sneaking a glance back, he saw that Anne and her mother each had one glove on. The pastry was already devoured, not a crumb wasted. Anne's sunken eye's held Emil's. *Thank you* she mouthed. Emil nodded slightly before turning away.

He was at the park when he heard the engines of the *Luftwaffe*. He fell with his back to the snow; bare hands shoved deep into his pockets and gazed up to the sky.

They were so amazing: shiny, metal birds of prey with a black, German swastika painted on the tail. They numbered in the hundreds; so many Emil couldn't count them all before they flew out of view. When he watched the *Luftwaffe*, he could forget about the quiet streets, the emptying store shelves, the blackouts.

He could forget about Anne Silbermann's haunted expression and frostbitten fingers.

When Emil watched the *Luftwaffe*, he easily believed that Germany's air fleet was the most powerful in the world. One day he'd be in the air flying an airplane, not on the ground staring at the sky, wishing. One day.

Chapter Twelve

*T*he land in Poland needs farming. We need more workers. We will send the Jews.

This was what the newspapers said. It didn't seem right or fair, but Emil supposed it made sense, especially if there weren't enough Germans to do the job. The Nazis had been relocating Jews for some time now, so when the trains arrived in Passau, most people took little notice.

Emil and Moritz happened to be walking by the station as the soldiers were loading them up. Emil hadn't realized how many Jews made their homes in Passau and the outlying regions. There were hundreds, with just the clothes on their backs and one small suitcase each. All of them leaving their homes and every material thing they owned that didn't fit in that one case.

Irmgard and Elsbeth were on the sidewalk ahead of them. Moritz poked Emil motioning for him to cross to the other side of the street. The boys watched as Irmgard and Elsbeth pointed at the Jews. Emil could tell by the way Irmgard twisted her face that she had said something mean. Then she puckered her lips and spit on the street.

Emil couldn't believe he once thought she was pretty.

Anne and her mother were in line. Their faces were thin and pale and etched with emotion. Sadness? Fear? Anne saw Emil with his friends, but pretended not to.

Emil felt bad that they had to leave this way, but at least they could start a new life in Poland. At least they no longer had to shovel snow in Passau.

In the three months from April to June 1940, Germany invaded Norway, Denmark, Belgium, Luxembourg, Holland and northern France. It seemed nothing could stop the advances of the German army.

The school buzzed with excitement.

"I thought Hitler promised not to invade the lowlands," Moritz muttered to Emil and Johann.

"It must've been necessary," Emil said. "Or they wouldn't have."

Johann scoffed. "Do you really believe that?"

Emil shrugged. He didn't know what to believe anymore.

In the classroom Herr Bauer shouted, "We are the victors!" He jumped up and down and clapped his hands like a child in the playground.

"Now we have Paris! Soon all of France will be ours! It's inevitable. I have pictures to show you." Herr Bauer passed around black and white photos of the French army.

"See, how pitiful? Their tanks are so weak and small. They can hardly roll over a stone without tipping. And do you see the uniforms, how womanly?"

He laughed and the class with him. Or most of the class laughed with him. Moritz and Johann barely broke a smile.

Rolf raised his hand. "How could France be so ill-prepared? Surely, the French knew the German Army was getting ready to invade."

"Indeed," Herr Bauer agreed, "we never hid our weapons. Anyone could see them in the parades, how modern and advanced they are."

"I'm so excited," shouted Irmgard out of turn.

Herr Bauer let it pass. "One day we will reign in all of Europe from the west to the east."

"At this rate," Friedrich jumped in, "we'll take over the world just as the *Fuehrer* promised!"

Really? Emil wondered. *What would they do with the whole world?*

Afterwards, in the schoolyard, Rolf made an announcement: All the boys from *Deutsches Jungvolk* and Hitler Youth would go to a summer camp for three weeks. "Heinz will tell you more," he said. "I'm so excited I just couldn't keep the news a secret!"

"Summer camp?" said Moritz, wrinkling his nose. He stumbled over a stone jutting out of the ground.

"Not just any summer camp, klutz," cut Rolf. "We're preparing to fight the greatest battle ever known. We must learn how to do our part to gain the ultimate victory!"

He shoulder nudged Moritz, and laughed. For the second time Moritz regained his balance before falling. "Even you, klutz," he shouted, loud enough for everyone in the schoolyard to hear, "will have to do your part." With the confidence of a tall, blond Aryan, Rolf sauntered away, his adoring fans flocking.

On Sunday afternoon a knock on the door interrupted Emil's parents' coffee time. Father and Mother exchanged nervous glances as Mother moved to answer the door. She couldn't restrain her surprise when she saw her brother on the other side. Onkel Rudi was a pilot in the *Luftwaffe,* which automatically made him Emil's hero.

"Rudolf?"

Onkel Rudi and Mother exchanged awkward hugs. Father rose to greet him and offered a stiff handshake.

"Leni," he said to Mother. "You look terrific."

"Thank you. You look very good yourself."

Onkel Rudi was a tall man and wore a crisp, white shirt under a bluish, gray tunic with a row of smooth, aluminum buttons down the center. On his head was a sharp-looking, peaked cap with the nation's emblem embroidered on it: an eagle with wings spread wide, a white swastika in its claws.

Emil and Helmut stood with mouths wide, enamored.

Onkel Rudi studied them, too, lips pulled tight in a straight line. He saw Helmut, a scrawny, young boy with his hair greased over to one side and Emil, a lanky, twelve-year-old youth.

Then he smiled and extended his hand. Emil knew then and there that Onkel Rudi was everything he wanted to be someday.

"Please, come join us." Mother motioned to Emil, "Go get another chair."

"I'm sorry to intrude."

"We're delighted to have you here, Mother said with forced cheerfulness. "Could I pour you a cup of coffee?"

"I would like that."

"I'm sorry that we don't have any cake today."

"Coffee is fine."

Cake was traditionally served with coffee on Sundays, but that had ended when the war began. Emil missed his mother's chocolate torte the most.

Polite conversation ensued, and it wasn't hard for Emil to tell that his parents and his Onkel viewed the world from opposing sides. Onkel Rudi was an adventurer, a world traveler. Emil couldn't recall Father ever saying he'd been outside of Germany.

"So, Peter," Onkel Rudi said, "have you joined the party?"

That explained the unannounced visit. His Onkel Rudi wanted his parents to join the National Socialist German Workers' Party. Joining would make their Nazi status official.

There was an uncomfortable pause.

"Peter..."

Father cleared his voice, cutting Onkel Rudi off. "Not yet."

"Well, you should do it soon. I know you'd hate to be in a position where you couldn't take care," he looked at Emil and Helmut, "of your family."

"Rudi," Mother said, her eyes imploring. Emil knew she didn't want to talk about this in front of him and his younger brother.

"I'm sorry, Leni. I just wanted to remind you of the importance of becoming members, before it's too late. I trust you've just been busy."

Onkel Rudi then launched into an articulate and affectionate description of the first-line military aircraft he flew, the Junkers Ju 87 dive-bomber, the Heinkel He 111 twin-engine bomber, the Messerschmitt Bf 109 single-engine fighter and the Bf 110 twin-engine fighter.

But when he brought up the fight in Poland, Emil knew there would be trouble.

"With the Me 109 fighters, we swept the pathetic Polish air force from the sky, like little bugs," Onkel Rudi boasted. Emil's parents were mute.

Onkel Rudi continued, "I flew the Ju 87 B, a deadly dive bomber," he spread his fingers out to mimic a plane and pulled his hand through the air. "Rat-tat-tat-tat! We destroyed their military bases. What a thrill to see Warsaw burn!"

Helmut's eyes were wide, and Emil could feel that his were round with wonderment, too.

"Rudolf! That's enough," Mother scolded.

"What? These are exciting times, Leni. Your kids will watch Hitler make Germany great again!"

To Emil's dismay, Father excused him and Helmut from the room.

"But Father," Emil protested.

"Do as you're told."

They climbed the stairs, just out of sight.

Father's voice drifted up. "How are we going to Germanize Poland, as you say? Less than ten percent of the people there are Germans."

"I admit, it is a formidable task," Onkel Rudi said, "but over time, the Poles will be moved out and replaced with proper Germans."

"Where are we going to find these Germans? We're suffering a shortage with the land we already possess. And what on earth are we going to do with four million Poles?"

"There are plans."

Silence.

Mother's voice didn't carry like Onkel Rudi's, but Emil could tell she was upset.

Then Onkel Rudi said, "Did God provide jobs for the German people? No, the *Fuehrer* did. Will God make the Fatherland a great nation? No, but the *Fuehrer* will."

Mother wouldn't like that, Emil thought. She spoke softly; he couldn't make out what she said.

Again, Onkel Rudi spoke, "Leni, those were fine beliefs for when we were children, but now we must let childish things pass."

Father spoke. "I'm sorry that we must disagree."

"As am I."

Chair legs scratched the floor. Onkel Rudi's voice. "It's time for me to go."

Footsteps to the front door.

60

"It was good to see you again, Leni. And you as well, Peter. Thanks for the coffee. *Heil Hitler*."

Emil and Helmut moved quickly and quietly to their rooms. Emil wondered if Onkel Rudi would ever visit them again.

Chapter Thirteen

"Emil!"

Emil could tell by his mother's tone that was about to put him to work.

"I'm busy, mother," he called back." He quickly changed into his *Deutsches Jungvolk* uniform and before his mother could challenge him again, he hopped on his bike pointing it in the direction of Johann's farm.

He dodged the potholes along the way; an early morning spring rain had filled them with brown, soupy water and he fought the urge to ride through, imagining the wide, murky wakes that were sure to soak his trousers. It was fine to leave a *Deutsches Jungvolk* meeting covered in mud, but a serious offense to show up that way.

The driveway to the Ackermann farm was long and narrow. The cinderblock house was small for five people, and there used to be six. Grandfather Ackermann died of heart failure on January 30, 1933, the same day Adolf Hitler was named Chancellor of Germany. Johann was positive the two events were linked.

Emil thought that was ridiculous. Hitler as Chancellor was the best thing that had happened to Germany.

Wasn't it?

He knocked on the front door and Johann's mother answered.

"Hello, Frau Ackermann. Is Johann here?"

"Yes. He is practicing violin with his father." Emil could hear the sweet sounds of strings perfectly tuned coming from the far room.

"Just wait, I'll get him."

The music stopped abruptly, and soon afterwards, Johann lumbered out.

"Hey, Johann."

"Emil, what're you doing here?"

"I had some extra time, thought I'd go with you to pick up Moritz."

"Okay."

Johann slipped into his jacket and walked along side Emil.

"Sorry, to interrupt your practice." Emil said. "You and your father are very talented. You don't know what torment I go through when Helmut pounds the piano."

"We have to learn new songs now, because of," he made a face, "*the Jewish problem*. How can anyone who wrote *The Three Penny Opera* be culturally deficient? It's all a load of manure."

"Johann!" In his mind Emil saw Herr Jäger jumping out of the bushes, pushing his spectacles up his shiny little nose yelling *Aha!*, then grabbing the both of them by the ears and dragging them to the *Gestapo*.

Johann just lifted his shoulders, apparently not bothered by the same nightmares.

Johann's sister was hanging wet laundry on the line; white sheets attacked her, and then scooped up with the breeze like sails. When they floated back down, the descending sun cast her in silhouette, like a shadow puppet.

"Emil?" Johann snapped his fingers. "Why are you staring at my sister?"

"I- I'm not," Emil stammered. A red flush crept up his neck unbidden.

"You better not. Anyway, Katharina's too old for you."

"Only one year."

"Shut up!"

Idiot. Emil wanted to punch him. Anyway, his sister looked like a boy.

Emil pushed his bike as he walked. One of Johann's bike wheels had popped, and the Ackermann's didn't have the money to fix it. When the boys got to Moritz's house they knocked on the door. Moritz answered it, still dressed in his school clothes.

"What are you doing here?"

"Thought we'd walk together to *Deutsches Jungvolk,*" Emil said. "Where's your uniform?"

"I'm not going."

"What?"

"I'm not going. It's no fun for me. I'm sick of getting picked on."

"But you have to go," Emil insisted. "They'll fine your family if you don't."

"Then I'll pay for the fine. I'm not going."

Johann was concerned, too. "Heinz is going to tell us all about the summer camp."

"Doesn't matter. I'm not going to summer camp either."

He closed the door and left his friends standing on the porch, dumbfounded.

Once out of earshot Emil said to Johann, "He may not go to *Deutsches Jungvolk* today, but you can bet your last *Reichsmark* that he will be going to summer camp."

"*Klar,*" Johann said, nodding.

They left for summer camp in mid-June. Actually, they found out later that it wasn't just summer camp, it was summer *labor service* camp. A title like that would send chills down the strongest spine, and Emil looked ahead to the next three weeks with a measure of foreboding.

Which was stupid. They'd be fine.

He said goodbye to his family and stoically shook Helmut's hand, thankful that it was he, and not his brother, who was being sent away.

Father gave Emil's hand a firm shake, his jaw clenched with emotion. "Be safe, son."

Mother didn't bother to restrain her emotion. Tears ran down her cheeks and she squeezed Emil tightly.

"I'll be home in three weeks, Mother. I won't be gone forever."

"I know. Just be careful, and come back to us in one piece."

Moritz and Johann were standing with the *Deutsches Jungvolk* unit at the train station when Emil arrived. They did indeed look like a group of young boys prepared for summer camp. They wore brown summer uniform shirts, black shorts and hiking boots. Each had a pack with their personal belongings on his back. There were smiles and laughter and pats on the back; Emil would have thought they faced a summer of swimming, games and camp songs. If he hadn't known better.

"I've never been on a train before," mumbled Moritz. Johann and Emil nodded, they hadn't either. Most of the boys had never been out of Passau before, especially not without their parents. The seats were hot where the sun beat on them and they burnt the back of Emil's bare legs. Though none of the boys was smoking, the smell of tobacco hadn't disembarked with the last group of travelers.

The stress induced chatter died away and Emil watched the town of Passau slip out of sight; the chug and rumble of the train vibrated the metal trim against his calves and he shifted to get comfortable.

Heinz made an effort to rally everyone, insisting that they all sing. *Rah, rah, rah* for Germany.

It was a less than stellar effort but it worked to pass the time. Soon they arrived at a station in the mountains; Heinz indicated that this was their stop.

But it wasn't the end of the journey. Five Krupp army trucks with canopy-covered decks were parked on the side of the road.

"Everyone, get into the back of a truck!" Heinz yelled.

Emil climbed vying for a seat near the opening at the back; he needed air. His guts churned and he felt a shimmer of moisture form on his hot forehead. Summer heat, or nerves, Emil wasn't certain. The engine roared to life and the driver shifted into gear. A wake of dust frittered across the pavement.

Moritz and Johann didn't look so good, either, Emil thought. Dark patches formed under their arms, and Johann's fists were tight, his knuckles stretched white. The mountainous roads twisted and turned, and Emil's stomach with it. *This must be what is meant by travel sickness*, Emil thought. His stomach hurt and the blood drained from his face. He hoped he didn't barf out the back.

"Are you sick, Emil?" Johann leaned over.

"It's just the ride. I'll be fine once we get there."

Johann nodded and held his stomach tighter, too.

Finally, they turned down a gravel road and the truck tires kicked dust in their eyes. Emil rubbed them clean and when he looked up, he saw the sign.

WE ARE BORN TO DIE FOR GERMANY.

They had arrived.

Chapter Fourteen

They herded everyone like cattle into a rectangular stone hall. The Passau youth were not alone—Hitler Youth and *Deutsches Jungvolk* groups from all over Bavaria were gathered together. Emil pushed in a little closer to Johann and Moritz.

They sat on long benches situated on either side of equally long tables. The scent from the kitchen wafted into the place, sausages and fried potatoes Emil guessed, but it didn't trigger his usual appetite. The motion sickness lingered and he felt bile creep up his throat. What he wouldn't give to stretch out on one of these benches and groan freely.

Officer Vogel, who was in his early twenties and as expected, tall, blond and fit, was the camp leader and called them to attention. He was quick to get to the point.

"You will learn to love the virtues of being a good soldier," he said. "You will esteem to the highest level of cleanliness, tidiness, teamwork and obedience. These requirements are non-negotiable and anyone not complying will be punished."

Emil observed two types of boys: those with an eager glint in their eyes, an excited blush of red in their cheeks who had difficulty sitting still; and those with stiff expressions, mouths twitching with apprehension who, though they may really want to serve the Fatherland, were already beginning to miss their mothers.

There were three brothers sitting across from Emil who belonged in the first group. Emil guessed them to be twelve, fourteen and sixteen, all with dirty, blond mops of hair and gray eyes that sparkled. Emil realized with a shock that he belonged to the second group. All he wanted right now was for his mother to tuck him into bed and bring him a warm bowl of chicken soup.

"Each week has a motto," Officer Vogel continued. Week one: *We fight*! Week two: *We sacrifice!* Week three: *We triumph!*

The hall erupted with choruses of *"Heil Hitler!"* and type one shouted the loudest.

Then Emil saw Moritz and Johann's grim expressions and realized that there was a third type. A small group of two that wasn't buying any of this at all.

After they ate, Officer Vogel took everyone on a tour. He showed them the playing field for sports and the rifle range and Emil thought that maybe summer camp wouldn't be so bad. Then he showed them a shed full of shovels and pointed to a field of hard dirt and rocks. "Here you will learn to dig trenches and fox holes," he said and Emil changed his mind.

Last he directed the youth to the lavatory and their sleep cabins. The room was sparse with only wall-to-wall bunks with perfectly made beds. It smelled like disinfectant. He left them to claim their own beds and Emil quickly chose his, wasting no time to get flat on his back, a mouse-like moan escaping his lips.

"It's only three weeks," Moritz mumbled, taking the bed next to him.

Johann climbed up on top of Moritiz's bunk. "I didn't see a beach," he said.

"Or girls," Emil added. "Some vacation."

It was a joke, but no one smiled.

The light-haired brothers were among them. Tobias, Jörg and Marcus Schindel. Turned out Tobias was their cabin leader. *Great*, Emil thought sarcastically.

"Young soldiers," he called out. "We are required to do ten laps around the sports field before *Abendbrot*. We are to meet Officer Vogel in precisely five minutes."

At least Emil was feeling better and the mention of the evening meal to come made his stomach growl. Ten laps wasn't so bad. It wasn't like they weren't used to it.

They were in bed by 20:00. Not so early when you knew the wakeup call came just after dawn. Emil laid on his back in the dark in the mandatory silence. He had never been away from home before and surprised himself with sentimental thoughts of his family. His throat felt tight, and he worried about the moisture that formed around his eyes. He wished he were tough and zealous like the brothers Schindel. Sometimes he even envied the unwavering devotion of Friedrich and Wolfgang, if only they weren't such idiots.

Emil could hear Jörg in the bunk above him, snoring; not a worry or longing to keep him awake. He let out a long sigh and waited for sleep to come.

The horn blew at 05:00. Emil and the rest of the boys had half an hour to wash up and make their beds. At 06:00, they carried their mess tins, mugs and cutlery to breakfast. After breakfast, they cleaned up again, and then they went on a morning hike followed by some kind of sport.

Just like on all their hikes with Heinz, Emil hung back with Moritz and Johann for the first while, all of them knowing that he and Johann would break away at some point and leave Moritz with the slower movers at the back.

Friedrich always started off easy so he could show them all how fast he could sprint. Even with a slow start he would make it to the finish in the lead. He liked to slap everyone from his own unit on the head as he passed by. Inevitably, he'd get Emil, Moritz, and Johann, three in a row. *Slap, slap, slap.*

"Hey!" Johann said.

"*Dummkopfs!*" He called them dumb heads.

"He's such an idiot," said Moritz.

"I'd like to give him a taste of his own medicine," said Johann, rubbing the burn from the back of his head.

They often took long marches though the hills with heavy back sacks, and this afternoon's march was no different. Moritz and Johann and Emil kept a steady pace near the middle of the pack, though Emil could hear Moritz's breath, quick and heavy. All of them were red faced and sweating in the afternoon heat. It smelled of dust and sweat, and Emil's mouth was swollen and prickly like his mother's pincushion. He reached for his canteen and took another swig of water.

Ordered rows of four youths snaked along a dirt road, with only the sounds of their boots marching in rhythm—*links, rechts*, left, right, until they had more blisters than clear skin on their feet, and every muscle in their bodies throbbed. This was their reasonable service, their duty and sacrifice. All for the love of their great nation and courageous *Fuehrer.*

Links, rechts, left, right. Emil still believed it.

Didn't he?

Officer Vogel suddenly shouted, "Enemy machine gun firing from the right!" After a slight pause, the first row threw themselves into the nearest ditch. They were all quick to catch on, rolling on the ground, bruising their bodies, scraping their bare knees. Emil groaned and wiped a trickle of blood off his leg. Johann rubbed his shoulder while Moritz laid flat on his back, just trying to catch his breath. Friedrich crouched low on his stomach, like a lion ready to pounce, waiting for the next command.

The muscles around Officer Vogel's mouth twitched like he was trying to hold in a grin. He called them back to formation. *Schnell, schnell.* Faster, faster.

He wasn't done playing. "Enemy plane flying low from the left!" and the youth repeated the dive as before into the opposite bank. Emil landed hard on his pack, the extra weight digging into his ribs. He clenched his jaw together, fighting the urge to cry out in pain. He understood now why his mother was concerned about his coming home in one piece.

Eventually, they came to a ravine, a shallow creek meandered along its floor, about fifteen meters down. Officer Vogel commanded them to line up single file.

"Since you have shown suitable aptitude on the rifle range," he began, his mouth still twitching, "you will prove your merit today by throwing a grenade."

A grenade? Emil thought, astounded. They'd had one session on the rifle range. One. His eyes widened, as did the others. Some with fear, some with frenzy.

The corners of Officer Vogel's lips tugged up slowly until he let out a bellow of laughter. "It's not a live grenade you imbeciles! They're dummies, for practice. *Mein Gott,* you should see your stupid faces."

Emil's shoulders sagged in relief, though he didn't join in with Officer Vogel's chuckles as some of the others, like Friedrich did. His lips pursed together in a displeased frown and he had to work hard to erase the emotion from his face.

They took turns throwing the dummy grenades as far as they could, pulling the fake cord before doing so. Officer Vogel was merciless towards the boys with weak arms and crooked aims.

Emil held the egg shaped dummy in one hand, surprised at how heavy it actually was. He felt sweat form on his upper lip as he tugged the cord and threw the grenade. His had landed across the ravine but not straight enough for Officer Vogel's liking.

"Girls! You're all a bunch of girls!" He rubbed his hands together before presenting the next grenade.

"I think we should try a real one." He handled it more gently than the others, convincing Emil that Officer Vogel wasn't joking around.

"This is a mark 4 grenade," Officer Vogel said, eyeing each boy in turn. "Who here is man enough to throw it?"

None of the boys dared to avert their eyes, but Emil was certain they all were thinking the same thing. "Don't pick me."

Officer Vogel's gaze settled on Wolfgang. At least he'd picked on one of the more athletic types.

Still, Emil caught the quiver in Wolfgang's arm as he reached for the grenade. Officer Vogel went over the procedure, which was simple. Pull the cord, then throw.

"Don't blow yourself up, Wolfe," Friedrich teased.

"Shut up!" said Wolfgang. He gingerly held the grenade in his hand.

Emil imagined Wolfgang pulling the cord and dropping the stupid thing, blowing everyone up.

"Come on Wolfgang," Rolf said, "throw it hard!"

Wolfgang pulled the cord and threw. His nerves were showing, and his toss was weak. The grenade just missed the lip of the ravine. Everyone gasped and ducked. The grenade rolled crookedly forward until it finally tipped over the edge, like a life and death game of golf.

It exploded.

It was thrilling and everyone cheered, even Moritz and Johann, happy that the first attempt ended well.

Now that the show was over, Emil hoped they could pack up and go back to camp. No such luck. Officer Vogel had a death wish. He presented another mark 4 grenade and with an evil grin, pointed at Emil.

It's simple, no problem, Emil thought, cheering himself on. He could do this. Officer Vogel handed him the grenade. Just holding that large, weighted, green egg in his hand made him sweat. Moisture trickled from his armpits under his uniform.

Suddenly, he felt nauseous. His earlier imagination of Wolfgang blowing himself up was now replaced with images of himself bursting into a million little, charred pieces. How could he throw this thing, with all this sweat? What if he dropped it?

"Throw it, you *Dummkopf*!" Friedrich yelled.

Emil would throw it all right. He wanted to throw it right at Friedrich's dumb head. He must have read Emil's thoughts, perhaps from the fiery glare Emil sent his way, because Friedrich actually shut up and took a step back.

Emil pulled the cord. Time seemed to slow down and his vision blurred. He was so sweaty and wet, he was sure he had wet his pants. *Throw it!* By some supernatural force Emil felt his arm whip over his head. The grenade followed a high, invisible arch, landing in the ravine with a *boom*!

The next morning after their hike, Officer Vogel called a game of soccer. He scanned the lineup of youthful faces,

his gaze quickly settling on the tallest boy.

"Friedrich, you will be captain of team one." A rapid decision brought him to his next choice. "Emil, you are captain of team two. Boys choose your teams."

Emil had never been the captain before and the idea, no, the reality, of it made him feel good. Important. And since Friedrich was the "enemy" captain, Emil really wanted to win.

Friedrich made his first call. "Wolfgang."

"Johann."

"Rolf."

Emil searched for another strong player. "Sebastian."

Down the row of boys they chose their team, each of them after the strongest and fiercest.

"You will be defeated," Friedrich taunted. "Like little puppies devoured by the wolves."

Emil would not lose to this idiot. His focus on building the best team was so intense that he missed Johann's perplexed look of disapproval until it was too late.

He'd forgotten to choose Moritz. He ended up on Emil's team anyway, but by default, not because Emil had chosen him. Moritz pretended not to be bothered by what had happened, but Emil knew him like he was his own brother. He'd hurt him badly.

Emil's excitement about the game diminished as he watched Moritz take the bench, his head bowed. Johann refused to go on the field, sitting next to him, his lips drawn tight.

As team captain, Emil tried to shake it off, calling his teammates to meet the challenge. He hated Friedrich even more now.

He wasn't surprised when they lost.

"Emil, you're such a little boy!" Friedrich boasted, strutting like a peacock all over the field, like winning a dumb soccer game made him a prince.

Moritz avoided him afterwards, and Emil never had a chance to say sorry. But what could he say that wouldn't make things worse? Moritz would hate to have his pity.

The mess hall smelled wonderfully of spicy sausages and fried potatoes, and Emil's stomach growled. He sat in his usual spot across from Moritz and Johann. The hall echoed with the chatter of boys, sprinkled with the odd hoot of laughter. This was typical for their table, too, on most nights, except for now: only cold silence from Moritz and Johann.

Emil should apologize, he knew that, but it felt so awkward to start. Moritz would eventually get over it, Emil reasoned. Tomorrow it would be like nothing had happened. He decided on small talk.

"Sure is hot out."

Moritz and Johann grunted.

Emil tried again. "This is great sausage."

The most Moritz and Johann would give were noncommittal shoulder shrugs.

Emil chewed his sausage and washed it down with tepid water. "Look, Friedrich is an idiot, okay?"

Together Moritz and Johann arched their eyebrows, looking steadily at him. Emil knew what that meant. They didn't think that Friedrich was the only idiot.

"I have an announcement!" Commander Riesling's voice rose above the chatter. "An incredible announcement!"

The din of the hall fell to silence. Emil placed his cutlery down in anticipation.

"The *Luftwaffe* just began an aerial attack on Britain!"

A loud cheer exploded from the youths in the hall. "*Luftwaffe, Luftwaffe!*" they chanted. Emil too, was caught up in the energy of it all. He loved the *Luftwaffe*. Johann and Moritz seemed shell shocked by the news. When they joined in with the applause, Emil could tell it was forced.

Later that night, Emil found himself alone with Moritz in the lavatory, scrubbing their faces clean.

"Hey," Emil said, grabbing at his chance to make things right. "About the game today, I just got caught up with Friedrich. I didn't mean..."

"Forget about it. It doesn't matter."

It did matter, Emil could tell by how he said it, but he let it drop. He rooted in his ears with a wet cloth, desperate to change the subject.

"So, that was something about the *Luftwaffe*, today. Maybe my Onkel Rudi was there."

Moritz looked at Emil like he was an alien. "Why did we have to attack Britain, Emil? Don't we have enough *Lebensraum* by now?"

Moritz finished his scrub down and Emil was left standing there, stunned by what Moritz had just said. They both knew that his statement was treason, punishable by hard labor or even death. All Emil had to do was report him.

Moritz knew it and Emil knew it. Was Moritz testing their friendship? Because of a stupid soccer game?

I can be either a good friend or a good Nazi, Emil thought. He knew now that he couldn't be both.

Chapter Fifteen

They survived summer labor camp, at least physically, and even their friendships had managed to stay intact. That was the thing about Moritz. He wasn't the type to hold a grudge. Emil was thankful for that. He couldn't stand having Moritz mad at him.

If labor camp was meant to turn him into a radical Nazi, it had failed.

Still, he wasn't prepared to abandon the cause entirely, either. How could he? He loved Germany, and would be faithful to the regime. What other choice did he have? He just had to figure out how to keep his friends happy, too.

They had a few languid summer days before the start of school. Emil figured it was only a matter of time before this false sense of calm would end. He was right.

The end came late on the evening of August 25. Herr Schwarz burst through the Radle's front door shouting, "Berlin's hit! Berlin's been bombed!"

His portly chest heaved as he delivered the news, stunning both of Emil's parents and Emil as well. *Britain's Royal Air Force had bombed Berlin? How had this happened?* Emil wondered. Propaganda Minister Joseph Goebbels had promised that not a single bomb would fall on Germany.

It turned out the bombing raid wasn't severe, but still, the whole nation was shaken. How did the enemy manage such a feat?

The bombing didn't stop Germany's own blitz in London. The *Luftwaffe* continued their attack on Britain and the radio and newspapers ceaselessly broadcasted the Fatherland's victory after victory.

At home, their efforts were focused on preparing for the coming winter. Emil and Mother worked the garden, gathering up the last of the potatoes, carrots, kohlrabi, beans and beets. All the women worked tirelessly to stockpile for their families, including Frau Schwarz.

Mother and Frau Schwarz often worked their backyard gardens together and Emil watched them as they paused, resting themselves against their hoes.

"Have you tried the 'Peoples' soap?" Frau Schwarz said. She brushed a blond wisp of hair off her forehead, tucking it under her gray scarf.

"It's terrible," Mother responded. "It's abrasive and smelly. It hardly produces any suds, no matter how hard you scrub. It's very hard on the clothing."

Mother had a light jacket on over her dress. The fabric had grown thin, the pattern faded. Emil couldn't recall her ever wearing anything but good quality clothes in the best condition. Even with a husband who worked at a clothing factory, she was unable to get a new dress.

A flash of anger burned his gut. He wanted his mother to have a new dress. He pushed the emotion away. *What was the matter with him?* Everyone had to make sacrifices.

Frau Schwarz nodded. "Now they want us to save the soap and use sand or soda to clean the house. Can you imagine?"

"How do we manage to keep *Kinder, Kirche* and *Kuche* these days?" Children, church and kitchen–this was the housewives motto.

"Can you believe the latest story about the house-wife?" Frau Schwarz rolled her eyes. "'Like a female bird, she pretties herself for her mate and lays eggs for him, while the male bird wards off the enemy.' I read it in the newspaper!"

Mother grew quiet, then in a near whisper added, "I'm afraid, Margarita. Our men will be recruited soon. So many men are dying every day. I don't know what I'd do without Peter."

Emil continued to dig potatoes, careful not to make noise that would remind them of his presence.

"I can't believe Hitler led us into another world war," Frau Schwarz said.

Emil stopped, surprised by the venom in his neighbor's words. *But Hitler had, hadn't he?* His parents had been right about that.

"Shh, Margarita!" Mother looked around. Seeing Emil seemed to startle her.

"I'm sorry, Leni. I shouldn't have said that out loud."

Helmut and Karl broke the awkward moment by running through the yards, Helmut tagging Karl with a loud, "I got you."

Emil picked up the basket of potatoes and headed for the cellar. The door was heavy and stiff and a waft of musty cold air assaulted his senses when he pushed it open. The steps were narrow and he peered over his basket, careful not to trip and tumble down. The cellar was small with a low ceiling and when Emil stretched, he was tall enough to touch the wooden beams with his head. Soon he would have to duck and hunch over like Father.

A row of jars lined the shelves. Tomatoes, yellow and green beans, apricot and raspberry jam, pickles, and canned fish from the river. With all the food mother had preserved over the summer and fall, they should be fine for the winter.

Emil poured the potatoes into the bin. It was half-full now. Full enough. He needed to get out, get away from his mother and Frau Schwarz and all their worries. He went to see Johann.

For a change the Ackermann house was quiet, no beautiful music escaping through the windows; his father was away with the orchestra. His sister Katharina was getting ready to leave for a meeting with the League for German Girls. She was a little taller than Emil, boyishly thin, and suited in the standard League for German Girls; long black skirt with a brown fitted blazer. Something about her intrigued him. He worried that he'd be caught staring at her again, so he shifted his eyes around the room, letting them land on her for only seconds at a time. Emil didn't have a sister, so having a girl wander around the room was new to him. Exotic and kind of scary, like having a peacock or panther living in your house.

Katharina said "hello" to Emil when she spotted him waiting for Johann. Emil waved shyly.

Johann joined them and Emil followed him out to the barn.

"What do the girls do in the League?" Emil asked once he was certain they were far enough away from Katharina that she wouldn't hear him. "Is it the same as *Deutsches Jungvolk?*"

"They hike and exercise," he said. "But mostly they talk about motherhood."

"Motherhood?"

"Yeah, they need to be good mothers to the Aryan race. That's why they need to be strong. My sister says they're taught to have a lot of children for the Third Reich."

"While their husbands are at war," Emil stated somewhat sarcastically.

"Actually, it's not necessary any longer to have a husband, just babies."

Emil raised an eyebrow. "What do you mean?"

"I mean, the Reich doesn't really care if a woman is married or not," Johann said.

Emil's eyebrows shot up.

"I'm not joking." Johann's face grew serious. "You can ask my sister."

Emil wasn't about to ask Johann's sister anything, especially not something like that. "I'm not exactly speaking to a lot of girls right now."

"If Irmgard has her way, you will."

"What are you talking about?" "I think she likes you."

"Who?"

"Irmgard."

"Likes who?" Emil asked.

"Man, are you stupid?"

Actually, Emil thought, she was looking at him a lot lately, and smiling with the flashy-eye thing. Thinking of her caused a warm blush up the back of Emil's neck. He dodged.

"Irmgard loves Herr Giesler. All the girls do."

"Girls can love more than one guy at a time, you know."

"How do you know?"

"It's common knowledge."

"Oh." Clearly, Emil had a lot to learn about girls.

The fact that they were a nation at war never stopped the town of Passau from setting up the traditional outdoor Christmas Market. Come late November, Crafters and merchants assembled their wares—breads, buns, candles, and glass and crystal ornaments—in Christmas themed kiosks. Cheery lights hung overhead and a group of singers filled the air with hymns and carols in three-part harmony. Usually everyone was eager to visit and mingle with a stroll through the market and a cup of warm, mulled wine in their hands.

It was a vain effort to forget. People didn't speak as freely or laugh as loudly as in previous years. The merchants' supplies dwindled quickly, and they offered careful apologetic smiles to those not fast enough at finding what they wanted.

The last Advent Sunday before Christmas arrived, and the Christmas market and all the town shops had closed. Everyone who could go to church went. Father was needed at the factory, so it was just Emil with Helmut and Mother.

"Hurry up, boys!" she admonished. Their boots crunched on the newly fallen snow as she prodded them toward the entrance of St. Matthew's Lutheran Church.

Moritz and Johann were there, seated with their families when they arrived.

St. Matthew's lacked the ornamental flare of the Catholic Church, and the pipe organ wasn't even in the same category. St. Stephen's had the largest pipe organ in Europe, taking up a whole wall. Emil thought their organ was a humiliation in comparison. Fraulein Post played it gingerly as everyone sang along; *hoch die Tür, die Tor macht weit*, Make high the door, throw the gate wide.

Pastor Kuhnhauser approached the podium adorned in his white clergy gown, a crimson scarf draped over his shoulders. A mural of the risen Christ was painted on the wall behind him, high above his head.

Helmut and Emil sat stiffly, not making a sound. They knew Mother would smack them on the side of the head on the way home if they disturbed the service. Johann and Moritz sat across the room stiff as posts, too.

"Dear fellow believers in our Lord Jesus Christ," Pastor Kuhnhauser began. "As we complete our observance of Advent let us reflect on how God our loving Father sent his son to be light in this dark world. Especially at this dark moment in history, may God be your comfort and light."

It was brave of him to call the war a dark moment, Emil thought. Or was it foolish? According to Nazi propaganda it was their brightest moment ever.

At that moment, the rear door opened. *Who would come so late to the service?* Emil wondered. They were apt to get Mother's eyebrow of disapproval. The small congregation shifted before gasping.

84

Black coats!

The SS had dared to enter a holy place. The sanctuary. Emil whipped his head to look back at Pastor Kuhnhauser, who blanched and swallowed. Emil imagined that this would alter his sermon somewhat.

Mother continued staring straight ahead, her shoulders pressed back, her lips pursed in an angry knot.

Even God's house belonged to Hitler now.

Chapter Sixteen

1941
MAY

The first months of 1941 crept by with simple routines. School, *Deutsches Jungvolk*, Mother making the most out of smaller quantities of food, Father working long hours, Helmut banging on the piano. And twelve and a half-year-old Emil had added a new routine: watching for Katharina Ackermann.

Katharina had the same blond wavy hair as Johann which she wore shorter than most young German girls. She looked to Emil like she would rather be wearing trousers, and he was sure she was capable of taking most boys in a wrestling match if she had to.

Chance had him peering out of his bedroom window early one February morning, when he'd spotted Katharina lugging a tin milk jug into town, obviously full by the way her body leaned heavily to one side. Emil assumed she was taking it to the market to sell. Something about the way her brow was furrowed, pure determination on her face as she went about her mission, drew him to keep watching her.

She wasn't anything like Irmgard or Elsbeth. Emil tried to put his finger on the difference. For one, Katharina didn't seem to care about how she looked, and Emil couldn't imagine Irmgard on an errand like this.

Every day she made the trip to the market with her heavy jug of milk, and every day Emil sneaked to the window to watch. As the seasons changed, she'd discarded her winter coat, her spring dresses revealing a more feminine figure than Emil had expected. Seeing her made his heart race. What was it about girls that caused that?

Or rather, this particular girl?

It was a warm day in May when Emil made his slip. The birds were causing a commotion–the swallows had built a nest in the roof, just above his bedroom window. Emil watched them and Katharina at the same time, which is why his reflexes were off. She noticed the birds, too and looked up.

She saw him. And waved.

Stunned and abhorring the thought of being caught watching her, Emil dropped to the floor. He remembered how mad Johann got when he thought he was watching her hang the laundry on the line that day.

Emil hoped she wouldn't say anything to him.

Yet, a grin tugged on his lips unbidden. She had *waved*.

On June 22, 1941, Germany invaded Russia. This seemed unbelievable at first because Germany had signed a non-aggression pact with the Soviet Union, yet more than three million German troops had lined up, stretching from the Arctic Circle, south to the Black Sea. It was no secret that Hitler hated the Communists and there was no shortage of propaganda spouting fear about a possible attack on Germany by them. A pre-empted strike made sense in light of that.

Even though Russia had the largest air force in the world, the surprise attack by the *Luftwaffe* crippled them. In just three days, more than 2,000 of Russia's planes were destroyed. Onkel Rudi was flying over there and Emil hoped he was okay.

When they heard the news, Emil's parents didn't say anything. He knew what they were thinking though: *Don't say anything around Emil.*

Emil felt like yelling, *I'm not going to report you!* but he kept silent. He couldn't be seen to take sides.

Next, Hitler bombed Moscow. When news of the *Luftwaffe's* huge success aired from the radio, Emil was divided. He still loved the *Luftwaffe*.

His parents were worried. Emil overheard them saying that many Germans thought the attack on Russia was a big mistake, even those devoted to the National Socialist Party. It's a big country. Surely they'll fight back. And besides that, no one had ever beaten the Soviets before.

What if they did fight back? What would happen to them then?

Then one day Emil, hopped onto his bike and headed to Johann's farm. It was mostly an effort to escape boredom because sometimes wartime was just plain boring. Frau Ackermann answered the door and to Emil's disappointment, told him that Johann wasn't there.

"Where is he?" Emil asked.

"With Moritz." Frau Ackermann frowned. "They've been spending a lot of time together lately. I hope they're not getting into trouble."

They've been spending a lot of time together? Without me? Emil wondered.

"If you see him," Frau Ackermann said as Emil turned to go, "tell him to come home. He has chores to do."

Emil rode directly to Moritz's house. It was quiet when he got there. No sign of Moritz or Johann in the yard. He knocked on the door not expecting his mother to answer as he knew she'd be at work. Mothers didn't normally work outside the home, but because she was a widow, it was acceptable. When Moritz didn't answer either, Emil turned the knob and let himself in.

"Moritz?" he called softly. Emil considered Moritz's house a second home, he'd been here tons of times, but no one had turned on the lights since dusk descended and the shadows were eerie.

It was weird to be in someone's house when they weren't there. Emil decided he'd check Mortiz's room and if he wasn't there, he'd hurry out again and just go home.

Emil quietly took the steps up to Mortiz's room in the attic, unconsciously avoiding the ones he knew from experience would announce his presence with a loud creak. If Moritz and Johann were up to something, he didn't want them to know he was there until he could see what it was.

The door was ajar just a fraction. Through the crack Emil saw his friends huddled around the desk. He could hear talking, not from them, but from a radio.

Why were they listening to the radio like that? Had another German city been bombed?

"What's going on?" Emil said walking in.

Moritz and Johann both jerked back, startled. Moritz quickly turned the knob, cutting the program off.

"Emil?" he said with odd stiffness. "What are you doing here?"

"Johann's mother said you were together. What are you guys doing?"

"Nothing," Moritz said too quickly. "Nothing much."

"You were listening to something on the radio. Why did you turn it off?"

Johann and Moritz gave each other strange looks. Johann went to Moritz's bed and lay down. Moritz stuffed his hands in his pockets and stood awkwardly in front of his desk, like there was something there he didn't want Emil to see.

Which made Emil want to see what was there even more. Mortiz stiffened as Emil walked toward him. "Emil?"

"What is the matter with you guys? You're acting crazy."

Then he saw the radio. It didn't look like anything he had seen before.

"What is it?"

Moritz took a deep breath and looked a Johann. "We might as well tell him." Johann nodded, okay.

"Tell me what?" Emil's mind raced. What could Moritz and Johann be hiding from him? And the bigger question was why?

"It's a radio," Moritz said.

"I can see that," Emil replied impatiently. But it wasn't the standard utility radio that was permitted by the Nazis that could only pick up German news reports.

Moritz continued, "It's called a Rola. It has *shortwave*. My brother brought it back from Holland."

"Does he know you have it?"

"No, I found it in his room. I didn't mean to..." he shrugged. "Anyway, it runs on shorter wavelengths than German radios."

"What does that mean?"

"With short-wave you can pick up Britain. The British Broadcast Corporation gives news reports in German, because they know people here are listening."

Whoa, Emil thought. "But that's illegal."

"Yes" Johann broke in. "We know."

Moritz handed Emil a piece of paper marked with his handwriting. "Here, look at this."

Germans suffer heavy casualties...

"What is this?" Emil said, dread creeping steadily up his chest.

"We heard it on the BBC. I wrote it down."

Emil read more. "But, it can't be true. It's completely opposite to our military broadcasts." He tossed the paper back onto the desk. "It must be propaganda."

"Propaganda? I'll tell you propaganda." Moritz stabbed the paper with his finger. "Our troops march into Russia, and the number of 'enemy' soldiers killed or captured, according to our military report, is phenomenal, but no mention is made of our own losses."

"Listen, Emil," Johann sat up on the bed. "It doesn't make sense. They have guns. They must be fighting back. The British reports give their own casualties, too, not just the enemy's."

Emil slowly sat down on the chair vacated by Johann. "Why didn't you guys tell me about this?"

"To be honest," replied Moritz. "We didn't know for sure if you could handle it. You seem really, well, taken in by, uh, everything."

Because I wanted a better Germany? Emil thought. *How was that wrong?*

"I'm not going to turn you in, if that's what you're worried about. You guys are my best friends, no matter what. But are you sure? Are you really sure?"

"You can hear it for yourself if you want."

91

What if it was true? What if the German people were being fed a pack of lies on their state commissioned people's radio? Emil almost didn't want to know. Life was already hard enough.

Emil felt his head nodding, but his heart raced. He knew listening to enemy broadcasts was strictly forbidden. When the BBC tones came through the cracking reception, he could barely hear because of the blood pulsing through his ears.

The BBC reports completely contradicted everything Emil had ever heard. They provided battle details from all sides. The German news reports said they had light casualties. The BBC said the German army had lost hundreds of thousands.

Emil didn't want to believe it. "They're lying!"

"Really?" Moritz challenged. "How can it always be so good for Germany, and always so bad for everyone else?"

"Britain is our enemy. They know some treasonous Germans will listen to illegal radio. They can say anything. Doesn't mean it's true."

Johann countered, "But what if it is?"

"It just can't be."

"Why?" Johann said. "Because you don't want it to be? Is that enough for you?"

"It can't be true." Emil covered his face with his hands. "Because if it is, we are in so much trouble."

"Emil," Moritz said softly. "I'm afraid we are in trouble."

Emil groaned. "Everything we've believed, wrong?"

"It's not the first time you've thought it, though," Moritz said. "Is it?"

No, it wasn't. Terrible little thoughts had often wormed through Emil's mind, thoughts that he tried to beat down, push away. Terrible, tortuous thoughts that grew more frequent and frightening as the months passed by. Terrible, treacherous thoughts. Doubts. About Hitler and the Reich. He remembered what they did to Anne, to Frau Kreutz and to Elsbeth's parents. He'd hoped that if he ignored them long enough, maybe the horrible little thoughts would go away.

"Does anyone else know about this?" he asked. His chest felt so tight he could barely breathe.

The two boys shook their heads.

"Good, that's good. We can't tell anyone. We'd be arrested."

Johann said, "Let's not do anything for now."

Emil and Moritz were quick to agree with that.

Listening to the BBC at Moritz's became like an addiction for the three of them. Emil's parents never asked him what he was up to. They had learned not to question his activities with *Deutsches Jungvolk* and mistakenly thought that was where he went.

One time after the ten o'clock report ended, Moritz turned to Emil and Johann. "We need to do something."

"What do you mean?" Emil said.

"We need to get the truth out somehow."

"How?"

"Flyers. We can write out flyers and drop them in mailboxes and phone booths. People need to hear the truth."

"Do you know what you're suggesting?" Johann said. "We would be sent to prison if we were caught."

"Then we don't get caught."

The first time they did it, they just made small cards, with some bit of news. *Thousands of German soldiers dead in Russia. We're fighting an impossible war.*

93

With three cards stuffed in his pockets, Emil felt like he was holding that grenade again. He wanted to throw them off his body! Fortunately, it was a moonless night, and blackout conditions gave a fair amount of cover. He slipped into the lobby of an apartment block and delivered his cards. His stomach was in such a nervous state by the time he got home, his bowels had turned to water. Emil decided then and there he would never do that again.

But by the morning, it didn't seem so bad. And so their campaign for truth had begun.

Those of the Same Blood belong in the Same Reich. Make this land German for me again!

Banners with slogans such as these by Adolf Hitler covered every free wall and fence space in the center of Passau. The summer Emil turned thirteen, he was kept busy with *Deutsches Jungvolk* activities supporting the war effort. Hitler was coming through with his promise to the people about creating a greater Germany by colonizing the East.

This didn't keep the boys from meeting at Mortiz's room to write out flyers, to expose the truth, whenever they could find some free time.

"Where's Johann," Emil asked when he met Moritz for their next covert writing session.

"He'll be here." Moritz put the paper and pens out on his desk in preparation. As if on cue they heard the squeak in the stairs.

But that should've been their first clue, since Johann knew about the squeaky step, and always avoided it.

Johann had brought his sister! Emil's face mirrored Moritz's shocked expression.

"Are you crazy?" Emil spit out.

"Relax," Johann said, waving his arms about, not looking relaxed at all himself. "She knows."

"How does she know?" Moritz said pointedly.

"She found a flyer in my room. I was meaning to hand it out, but...."

Katharina stomped her foot. "Stop talking about me like I'm not here."

"It's very dangerous." Emil said, avoiding her eyes.

"I know the risks." Katharina said. "I agree with what you're doing and I want to help."

"But this is really dangerous," Emil said again. He didn't want anything bad to happen to her, not that he *liked* her or anything.

"Everything is getting dangerous," Johann added. "Access to the truth is more important now than ever."

"How many of you are writing out flyers?" Katharina asked.

"Three."

She smiled. "So, now there's four."

"Well, she's here now," Moritz said with a deep sigh. "And another writer would be helpful,"

Then he broke his own pact about not talking to girls and said to Katharina, "Okay, but you must swear, *swear,* to keep everything you see and do here an absolute secret."

"I swear," she said.

Their small cards gradually became larger, full-length pages, with nearly entire newscasts transcribed. They didn't have a typewriter, or a way to make copies, but they each committed to writing out three by hand and finding new places to drop them. It wasn't much but it felt good to do

95

something right, and maybe something good would come of it.

They never went out together. They always made their deliveries alone, and always in a different part of town. They had also made a pact. If one of them was caught, he or she, (*God forbid*, thought Emil) wouldn't implicate the others. As far as anyone else was concerned, they each acted alone.

After awhile, Emil lost his sense of fear. *Who pays attention to a piece of paper falling from the pocket of a boy?* But the news of these "works of treason" had spread through the SS, and one day as Emil felt the paper slip from his fingers, he felt a strong hand gripping his shoulders.

"*Halt*, boy!"

The SS officer had something in his hand. It was his paper!

Emil swallowed hard and remembered his vow to his friends. He worked alone.

"You dropped this," the officer said.

"Yes, sir."

"We must not litter the Fatherland. Surely your parents and teachers have taught you that much."

Emil couldn't believe his luck. The SS officer didn't even open the paper, just handed it back to him.

"So sorry, sir," Emil stammered. "It won't happen again."

"Agreed," he said. "*Heil Hitler!*"

"*Heil Hitler!*"

Chapter Seventeen

1942
JANUARY

The end of nineteen forty-one saw the beginning of the Second World War. Japan attacked Pearl Harbor. America and Great Britain declared war on Japan. Germany and Italy declared war on America.

And the Jews left in Germany had to wear a big, yellow six-pointed Star of David on their jackets.

Emil wandered the streets of Passau, teeth chattering, fingers burning with cold. He stuffed his hands deep into his pockets, his steps short and quick. No one and nothing was warm; even the towers of the Cathedral appeared barren and ashamed.

His mind took him to all the places he didn't want to go: to the war, always the war, and how deep down inside he didn't think they would win; to Helmut, and how he wished his little brother could have a carefree childhood. That they all could have that.

As bad as those thoughts were, they were better than dwelling on the raw, aching pang of hunger that throbbed in his gut.

"Emil!"

He turned to find Katharina running to catch up to him.

"Hi," he said. A strange discomfort settled over him. He'd never been alone with Katharina before. They were always together with the gang.

Katharina buried her red nose into her scarf. Her hair was longer now, braids sticking out from underneath her wool hat. She had the telltale signs of early mal-nutrition—gray circles under her eyes and sunken cheeks, and her face was bright red from the cold. Despite that, he still thought that she was pretty.

She didn't seem in a hurry to leave him. "Mother sent me to buy some flour for bread. Do you think there will be any left at the market?"

"I don't know. Doesn't hurt to check, I guess."

"It's cold." Katharina stated the obvious. "We'd be warmer if we ran. Do you want to race me?"

Anything was better than an awkward conversation.

"Sure, where to?"

"From here to the end of the street."

"Okay."

They took the pre-racing position. Emil decided he would go easy on her, make sure he didn't win by too much. They were both cold and hungry; he didn't need to add humiliation to that.

"Ready," she said, "set, go!"

He needn't have worried about humiliating her. Her legs moved liked wildfire, and it was Emil who was in danger of a humiliating loss. He pushed harder, his heart thumping wildly, first as a result of sudden exertion, second with the possibility that he might lose to a girl.

Emil managed to keep a slim lead and whether she let him win or not, he didn't know and he didn't want to know. They flopped onto a nearby bench, and she started laughing.

"Why—are you—laughing?" he puffed.

"Because it was fun, Emil," she said in between breaths. "I haven't had fun in a while." She smiled at him and Emil felt a big sappy grin take over his face in return.

"I'll walk with you to the market," he said, suddenly wanting to be with her for longer.

"Sure."

They entered the store and as expected the shelves were empty, the shop like a giant face with all its teeth knocked out. Emil wasn't sure why it remained opened. When a shipment of any kind came in, word got out like a strong wind and almost instantly a long lineup of people would form eager to buy anything they could get their hands on.

"I'm sorry, Katharina."

"I know."

Across the street they spotted Heinz. He had his arm around a girl, flirty and giggling, pushing up against Heinz's body to keep warm.

"Elsbeth will be so jealous," said Katharina. "She has a big crush on him."

Emil couldn't help staring. What would it feel like to put his arm around a girl? He imagined himself with his arm around Katharina. She would be soft and warm, comforting. Emil feared his face was doing strange things because Katharina suddenly addressed him. "Are you feeling okay, Emil?"

He feigned a cough. "Um, yeah, I'm fine. Just the usual. Hungry, cold."

"Yeah," she said, staring. "The usual." Then she took his hand and rubbed it, causing a strange but pleasant floating sensation to rise up in his belly.

Emil could remember when he never thought about hunger, except for that last half hour before dinner. Back then any sense of urgency was soon satisfied by a roasted pork and potato meal.

Meals like that were from another lifetime ago, a dream. They said it'd get worse before it got better, but Emil couldn't imagine it getting worse than this. The unending twisting, dull pain that sat in his stomach. It wasn't like they were starving to death, yet. They still had potatoes. When Mother called them for supper Emil raced to the table and it only took three or four bites to calm the angry, growling beast in his stomach before the potatoes began to taste like dust.

They say man cannot live on bread alone. He'd like to add potatoes to that.

It was after one such meal, potatoes, with a side of potatoes, with potatoes for dessert, that Mother and Father shared their news. Bad news.

"Boys," Mother said, "I have to go to work."

"What do you mean?" Emil said.

"She means away from home," said Father.

Away from home? This was difficult to comprehend.

"Like you, Father?" Helmut's face twisted, perplexed. "I thought only fathers went to work. Mothers stay home."

"Times have changed, son. War changes everything."

"What will you do?" Emil asked his mother.

"I'm going to work at the clothing factory."

"With Father? That won't be so bad. Even if you don't see Helmut and me as much, you'll have Father." Emil wanted to encourage her. She was so sad. "We'll be fine. I promise. We'll look out for each other."

Mother smiled, and Emil thought he'd worked his magic until he saw a big, shiny tear roll down her face. She and Father kept looking at each other and Father grabbed her hand.

"What? Is there something else?" Emil asked.

"Yes, son," said Father. "Boys, I won't be working together with your mother. You see, they've called me to service. I'm going to Berlin."

"You've been drafted!" Emil remembered the discussion that Mother had with Frau Schwarz in the garden long ago. How they worried about the draft. Even though Emil had felt troubled back then, he didn't really think it would happen. Not to their family. Not to Father. His chest tightened and he sighed heavily through his nose.

"Both you and Mother gone!" shouted Helmut. "That's not fair!"

"How long will you be gone, Mother?" Emil asked. He clenched his fists under the table, working hard to reign in his anger.

"Oh, I'm not leaving home, I'll just be working at the factory. But I'll be there a lot. I won't be around for you boys as much anymore."

Helmut looked like he might cry.

Mother started work the next day. Gone were the days of the German woman staying home to take care of house and family. Oh, a woman's place was still in the home, they were told, but since the whole of Germany was their home, they must serve wherever they could.

Father left soon afterward. It was a blur of tears with Mother and Helmut sobbing, but Emil was determined to stay strong. He would be the man of the house while Father was away.

"Please, Peter, come back to us," Mother pleaded. There was a herd of families at the station saying good-bye to their men, husbands and fathers, grown up sons. They loaded the trains, some with eager anticipation, others with much reluctance and sorrow. Like Father.

The train crept away from the station, and Emil and his mother and brother stood waving until they could no longer make out his father's face.

On the walk home, they passed a funeral procession. Another soldier killed in the line of duty.

Emil had a horrible thought: *did he just see his father alive for the last time?*

Chapter Eighteen

The meetings in Moritz's attic had to be moved when his mother grew ill and had to leave her workplace. The group decided to meet in the barn loft on the Ackermann farm. Herr Ackermann traveled a lot with the orchestra, and the place was empty as the farm help was fighting in Russia. Thankfully spring had arrived early, so they were warm enough in the drafty loft.

"Is it just me," Moritz said, "or is everyone looking a little...uh... skinny?"

"You calling me skinny, boy?" Johann said. The three boys were in the loft and Johann fell back into the hay chuckling. "I've never looked better a day in my life."

They laughed, but they knew the truth. Emil remembered at time when Moritz was a bit pudgy. Their thinness now was frightening. Their threadbare pants were held up by belts or rope.

"I saw Jäger's son," started Johann.

"Albert," Emil threw in.

"Yes, Albert. Back on leave from Berlin. He looked good. Almost fat."

"I saw him, too," Emil said, lying back to join Johann. He put his arms behind his head, pointy elbows sticking out like arrows. Moritz did the same.

"I'm so used to seeing pale faces, it was strange to see someone with rosy cheeks," Johann said.

Emil turned to him, noting the dark circles around his eyes.

"The troops get vitamins. At least that's what I hear," said Moritz.

"Potatoes have vitamins," Emil countered. "If you keep the skins on. Mother always keeps the skins on now."

"Yummy!" Johann snorted.

"I think my hair's starting to fall out," said Moritz.

"My teeth are," said Johann. "It feels like they're dissolving, like sugar cubes in a glass of water."

"So, how long do you think Albert's in town for?" Emil said. "If he's anything like his father, we're in trouble."

Silence.

Then fear.

Was it possible someone could hear them in the loft? Were they really that safe? Did Jäger have someone follow them? Albert?

"You know, in the future," Johann said, "dentists are going to pull teeth out through the nose."

"What?"

"Why?"

"Because nobody dares open his mouth."

More silence.

"See?" he said, sitting up to stare at Emil and Moritz. "It's a joke!"

They laughed. First out of nervousness then because it actually was funny. Their laughter was contagious.

"But, really, we should watch out for Albert," Emil said. "I think he's a weasel."

"We should watch out for everyone," said Moritz.

"I'm just glad we're not old enough to fight," added Johann. "And, it's not because I'm scared."

104

"I'm scared," Emil said.

"Me, too," Moritz agreed.

"Okay, I'm a little scared. But we should be safe tucked away in the far corner of Germany. Passau means nothing to the British or Americans."

"You're probably right, Johann," Moritz said. "We just need to wait it out."

"Dining on potato skins."

"Shh!" Emil whispered.

Moritz stiffened. "What?"

"I heard something."

Stillness. Then, hay crunching under footsteps. They barely breathed. The ladder to the loft shook.

"Boys?"

"Katharina!" they stammered in unison.

"You scared us to death!" Johann said.

"Never mind that, Johann." She climbed up and sat with them. "I have bad news."

"What?"

"Luebeck's been bombed."

Luebeck was a port city on the Northern Sea.

"That's terrible," Emil said.

"The town's on fire," she said. "The Royal Air Force is counting it as their first major victory."

"It wouldn't take much to burn Luebeck," Johann said. "The medieval part of town is built with wood."

"Still, it's proof that no place is safe," said Moritz. "It doesn't matter that we're not old enough for the draft. They're bombing cities, like they said they would. We're as vulnerable in our own homes as any soldier on the front lines."

The next day a letter from the headquarters of the Hitler Youth came in the mail addressed to Emil.

"What do they want?" Mother asked.

"They want me to attend glider camp! Glider camp, Mother!" His lifelong dream of flying airplanes was about to begin. He pushed from his mind the fact that the opportunity was coming from a source he now opposed.

"But Emil, you're only thirteen." She didn't share his excitement.

"I'm almost fourteen, Mother, and finally I will get to fly!"

"Emil, if you were meant to fly you would have been born with wings. May I see the letter?"

The camp was situated in the Rhön Mountains in Bavaria.

"What about school?" Mother said.

"Glider camp is only on weekends."

"You'll miss the Saturday classes."

"I'll study extra hard."

Emil humored her with this conversation, giving her the illusion that she had some say in whether or not he could go.

Glider camp was Emil's official entry into Hitler Youth and it felt good to leave the childish version, the *Deutsches Jungvolk* behind him. He breathed easier and felt something akin to joy. All the kids at glider camp were so passionate about flying and Emil's own enthusiasm for airplanes was a terrific cover for his secret revulsion of the Nazi regime. At glider camp, he could forget about everything else for awhile.

The School Glider 38, or SG 38, had a wooden open fuselage attached to a wooden skid underneath. The wings stretched out on either side and were braced with wires and small metal skids protected the wingtips if they touched the ground, which they did.

But they didn't learn to fly overnight.

In fact, each student spent many hours helping the others fly, before he would one day have a turn.

Gustav was sixteen and had been attending camp for more than a year. He needed to add to his time in the air to get a certificate for his next level.

Eighteen boys waited on the crest of the hill, watching as Gustav strapped on his helmet and then folded himself into the open cockpit.

He tapped on his helmet, a sign that he was ready, and the rest of the boys grabbed the thick, rubber rope, a gigantic slingshot.

Someone shouted, "Pull!"

Emil's face pinched with exertion as he pulled with all his strength, digging his heels into the ground.

"Release!"

Gustav catapulted into the air. He pulled back the stick and up, up he went.

"*Wunderbar!*" Emil shouted, along with the others. Wonderful.

It was a short flight. Gustav glided safely to the ground, and the boys ran down the hill to meet him. It was the job of the new kids to drag the SG 38 back up the hill, but Emil didn't mind.

For six glorious weekends, Emil took the train to glider camp. When they weren't catapulting an older kid into the air, the new group would catapult each other on level ground, so they could learn to balance the glider. They had to keep the wings off the ground before they were allowed to get air. It wasn't that hard, Emil thought, much like riding a bike. After a few tries, he barely touched the wingtips to the ground at all.

In April, Emil's Hitler Youth unit started Flak training. Emil would learn how to shoot planes out of the sky. Actual planes with real pilots flying them. Rolf, Friedrich, Otto, Hans, Wolfgang, Moritz, Johann and Emil were all there with Heinz, of course, at the helm. It felt weird not having Katharina around, Emil thought. She was with her girls' league unit, and she hated it. If there was one thing Emil agreed with National Socialism about, though, that was the policy that women should not bear arms. Though Katharina was one of the boys, sort of, she was still a girl. A part of Emil wanted to protect her.

This was a special training event and another unit from across town joined in, their leader demonstrating zeal to match that of Heinz's.

And for the first time, they met SS Officer Heimlich.

He wore a sharp-looking gray Waffen-SS uniform with a row of medals and ribbons pinned neatly above the right pocket and a Tank Destroyer badge stitched on his upper right arm. This meant he had destroyed at least one enemy tank using a hand held explosive.

Even Heinz seemed intimidated.

SS Officer Heimlich introduced the light Flak and medium Flak gun models. While a medium Flak took a large team to operate, a light Flak could be run by one person.

"This light Flak is equipped with a 12.7mm anti aircraft machine gun and 20mm towed cannons," he explained. He pointed to Heinz who proceeded to position himself in the seat that was low to the ground, his long legs reaching out in front of him. His left hand held on to a handle while his right hand rested on a grip attached to what looked like a large gear. A narrow cannon shaft, taller than a man, pointed to the sky.

"These guns are light," SS Officer Heimlich said, each word clipped and accentuated. "And can be set up quickly. They are fast firing and quite effective against aircraft flying at low altitudes.

"A capable Flak fighter will provide necessary protection for railroads, bridges, towns and coast-lines," he said, his mouth forming a grim line.

"Since Passau is a city where three rivers join and it has many bridges, this will be very important for us."

He peered at the boys seriously, "Now, it's your turn." He nodded at Heinz, who pointed to Rolf.

Rolf walked stiff and tall to the Flak gun and positioned himself in the manner demonstrated by Heinz. In fact, Emil thought, Rolf was looking more like his brother all the time: taller, stronger, and more arrogant.

SS Officer Heimlich instructed him on where to put his hands and how to shoot. Emil jerked back with surprise when a cannon shot into the air and exploded!

Rolf's stunned face expressed the worry they all felt. *Was Rolf in trouble?*

SS Officer Heimlich's stern face cracked slightly, a grin.

"Well, done," he said. "Next."

One by one they took turns, shooting Flak gun arsenal into the sky.

Emil watched nervously as Johann turned the handle, his strong arm bulging with the effort. Then Moritz. His eyes followed the orange streak that seemed to go on forever, but didn't look too impressed with his success.

By the time Friedrich's turn came, he was like a bulldog just let loose from his pen.

"Down with you, you dirty Allied dogs!" he yelled. SS Officer Heimlich seemed particularly pleased.

When it was his turn, Emil stepped up with feigned confidence, settling into the seat like the boys had before him. It was heavier than the others had made it appear. The cannon nose pointed straight up and Emil moved its weight toward an imaginary enemy. He turned the crank with his right hand and pushed the button to release fire.

Energy burst into the sky and back through his body. One day they would want him to shoot an Ally out of the sky. Could he do it? While he didn't believe in this war, would he fight anyway? How could he not? Emil felt an uncomfortable lump build in his throat.

SS Officer Heimlich nodded his approval and called for the next boy. Emil returned to his place in line.

They couldn't end the day without a public display of unified pride and importance. Both Hitler youth units marched through downtown Passau in unison, goose-stepping in perfect-metered time, right arms stretched forward, straight and stiff. The crowds stopped to watch and admire. *"Heil Hitler,"* they shouted. *"Heil Hitler,"* the boys cheered in return.

The army in Passau had set up several Flak stations on the outskirts of town, near the rivers. Emil couldn't believe it when Heinz directed him to man one with Friedrich. Eight hours alone with Friedrich and his ego would make him crazy for sure.

"We're immensely lucky to be alive and of age to fight in the German army," Friedrich said to him while puffing on a cigarette. "We may not yet be soldiers, but damn, we could quite possibly shoot an airplane out of the sky. Imagine that!"

Ever since their time on the playground, Emil knew that Friedrich loved to hit things. Or throw things. As long as the object broke something or was broken itself, or in some way injured a bystander, Friedrich was happy. His mother gave him trouble for breaking his toys or beating up kids in the playground. It got to the point where their arrival at the children's park caused a mass evacuation, Emil and his mother included. You could see the humiliation on Friedrich's mother's face but Friedrich had thought it was funny.

Operating flack must seem like the best of both worlds to him, Emil thought. Throwing cannons and hitting the Allies.

"I wish I was manning a Flak in Berlin," Friedrich said, after a seriously long moment of awkward silence. "Then I'd see some action!"

Emil raised his eyebrows, and Friedrich took it as encouragement to keep going.

"Imagine shooting down a dirty RAF dog?" He pointed the nose of the Flak at an imaginary plane and made *rat-at-tat* noises with his mouth.

"No one's ever going to come to Passau," Emil said, stifling a yawn. "We are in the dullest part of Germany."

"You are right there, *Kamerad*." Friedrich paced in a small circle. He fished out another cigarette from his pack, and lit up. It was his seventh this shift and they'd only been there for two hours so far. No wonder Friedrich was so jumpy. "Soon we'll be called to fight, then the fun will begin."

"Why are you so anxious to fight?" Emil said. "You got a death wish?"

"I want to fight, Emil, because I love my country." Friedrich said this like he was addressing a child. "The *Fuehrer* has a dream for a great and glorious nation, free

111

from vermin. Pure and strong. It's my dream, too. And if you want something bad enough, you must be a man and fight for it."

Emil stirred in his seat but didn't respond.

After a while, Emil said, "Aren't you hungry, Friedrich?" *Because of the war? Is this the promise of greatness?*

"Of course I am. Why do you think I smoke so much? Helps to dull the pain in my gut, takes my mind off the here and now, so I can focus on the greatness to come. You should try it, Emil. You want one?"

It was tempting. Emil's gut hurt, but he imagined himself taking a drag and then collapsing to the floor in a fit of coughing. Friedrich would love that and tell everyone. With embellishments.

"Thanks, but I'll pass," Emil said.

"Fine by me," Friedrich slipped the pack back into his pocket.

Emil tried to think about other things besides his hunger to pass the time and to block Friedrich out. What was there besides the war? There was their secret mission. And the fact that his father was in Berlin and they hadn't heard from him in weeks. Not much to ponder that didn't create a vice grip of anxiety in his chest.

Except Katharina. He thought of her a lot. She didn't know it, but they often passed the time together.

Chapter Nineteen

When Emil's shift ended at dusk and he could finally escape Friedrich and his ego, he rode his bicycle to the bus stop to meet Mother when she finished work. The streetlights were turned off due to the black out and Emil didn't want her walking home alone in the dark.

"Hello, son," she said after disembarking. Her shoulders were slumped and she sighed with fatigue. Emil pushed his bike alongside her slow strides in silence. All the things they never talked about—like Father in Berlin and if he was still alive, and how thin and weak they all were, especially Helmut who didn't seem to be growing—hung in the air between them.

He was waiting for them when they arrived home. Mother gave him a hug and told him to be careful and then, with heavy steps she went upstairs.

Helmut turned on the small flashlight in his hand. Emil handed over his bike, as Helmut didn't have one, so he could perform his duty to the Fatherland. His job was to ensure the blackout order was fulfilled and report any violators.

Emil's bike was too big for him, so he stood while riding, pushing ahead in the dark. Such a brave little boy, Emil thought.

113

It was Emil's observation that bad things happened in clumps. A string of mundane events—school, Hitler Youth, church, Flak duty—would be followed by the catastrophic. Just enough monotony to lull them into a slumber, to cause some of them to drop their guard.

This time it was Herr Schwarz. Early one morning Emil awoke to the pounding of fists on their neighbor's door. He peeked out his window and yelped. The Gestapo.

"Mother!" Emil shouted while running down the steps to get a better view out of the kitchen window.

"Emil! What is it?"

"There's trouble at the Schwarzes!"

They knocked their heads together vying to get a good look. No way would they actually step out doors; that would only lead to more arrests, and going to jail was not on Emil's list of things to do.

Frau Schwarz was frantic, crying, grabbing onto her husband's shirt, an action that was sharply reprimanded with the swat of a bat. Frau Schwarz whimpered in pain, holding onto her wrist as she watched them take Herr Schwarz away.

Every window on the street had the curtains pulled to one side with curious faces peering out. Frau Schwarz ran back inside.

"I'm going to her," Mother said. She pulled her housecoat together and slipped out the back door.

Later she told Emil the story: Herr Schwarz had made a joke. Of course, he was the type of person who liked to laugh, and thought laughter was a good medicine for troubled hearts. He said something unflattering about the *Fuehrer* to a co-worker, who promptly reported him.

"Margarite told him to lie," Mother said. "There were no witnesses to the conversation. Herr Schwarz didn't say

114

he would do it though. Margarite's not sure that he'll deny the truth to save himself."

Mother had always told Emil and Helmut that lying was a sin. But what the Gestapo was doing was a bigger sin. Herr Schwarz didn't deserve to go to jail for this. What would happen to Frau Schwarz and Karl now?

Emil didn't know if Herr Schwarz had lied or not, but they didn't send him to jail, they sent him to France. Not to work at an office job like Father. Herr Schwarz was sent to the front lines.

All of Germany's efforts had been turned to fighting the war. Because of this, Emil's days at glider camp came to a sudden and abrupt end. He almost cried. He didn't get his turn to fly.

Even the carefully controlled German press couldn't minimize this event. Two days later, the Allies bombed Essen. Johann, Moritz, Emil and Katharina talked of nothing else, and when George Orwell, with his deep rugged newscaster voice, addressed the citizens of Britain on the BBC, which was followed by a German translation, Moritz, Johann, Katharina and Emil were listening.

"On two days of this week, two air raids, far greater in scale than anything yet seen in the history of the world, have been made on Germany. On the night of the 30th of May over a thousand planes raided Cologne ..."

"Oh, my dear God," said Katharina.

"...during the autumn and winter of 1940, Britain suffered a long series of raids which at that time were quite unprecedented. Tremendous havoc was worked on London, Coventry, Bristol and various other English cities."

"I knew we were going to pay for that," Moritz whispered.

"The big bombers now being used by the Royal Air Force carry a far heavier load of bombs than anything that could be managed two years ago. In sum, the amount of bombs dropped on either Cologne or Essen would be three times as much as the Germans ever dropped in any one of their heaviest raids on Britain."

"Wow," Emil said, stunned. Like everyone in Germany, they had seen the propaganda photos of the damage done to London after the *Blitz*. Emil couldn't imagine what Cologne must look like now.

Orwell continued, *"... It should be noted that these thousand-plane raids were carried out solely by the RAF with planes manufactured in Britain. Later in the year, when the American air force begins to lend a hand, it is believed that it will be possible to carry out raids with as many as 2,000 planes at a time. One German city after another will be attacked in this manner."*

"City after city?" Emil said. "Is that possible?"

Moritz, Johann and Katharina's wide eyed shock reflected the same fear as he had. The broadcast ended and a thick silence filled the room.

Chapter Twenty

The first time Emil heard the name Helmuth Huebener was on August 11, 1942, the day after his arrest.

Earlier that day, Emil had passed a man tossing a paper into a trash bin. Emil stopped and picked it out. The headline read:

HITLER YOUTH GUILTY OF TREASON

Helmuth Huebener of Hamburg, a seventeen-year-old member of Hitler Youth was arrested for treason. He and three others were caught... a fist-sized lump formed in Emil's throat and he swallowed hard, *...listening to forbidden radio broadcasts and copying and distributing lies about the Reich.*

Emil tucked the paper into his jacket and ran all the way to the Ackermann farm. Johann and Moritz were there.

"We live in the southeast corner of Germany and they are all the way across the country in the north," Moritz said excitedly. "Doing the same thing as us!"

"But they got caught," Emil said.

"Yes, but it proves we're not alone," he countered. "Unless it's pure coincidence, it means there are others who are listening to foreign news and daring to spread the word."

"They were older than us," said Johann.

"So?" countered Moritz.

"So, I don't know." Johann shrugged. "I wonder how they got caught? I wonder what will happen to them now?"

They followed the story, the trial of the four lads in Hamburg, with much interest. They became known as the Huebener Group, and had been sent to the dreaded People's Court in Berlin to await their sentencing. News of the arrest and incarceration didn't subdue Emil and his gang, in fact it had the opposite effect. Knowing they weren't alone in their mission had stirred them up and instead of backing off, they went out every night to deliver more flyers.

Then, on October 27, 1942, Helmuth Huebener, the young Nazi resister from Hamburg, was executed. Moritz, Johann, Katharina and Emil were in the loft passing around another newspaper Emil had absconded.

"They chopped off his head!" Katharina said.

"I can't believe it," said Johann. "Prison yes, but death?"

"They're only kids," added Katharina, "not much older than us."

"Maybe we should take a break," Emil said. "You know, for a while."'

"No!" Moritz was adamant. "Now is the time to go harder, not slow down." He paced the loft almost bumping his head on the slanted ceiling. "Don't you see? People are listening. They may pretend not to agree, but the more people talk about it, the more likely they will see the truth!"

Emil sat across the loft from Katharina. He couldn't stand the thought of anything bad happening to her. "I hear what you're saying, but do we really want to risk prison?" Or worse? "I've heard stories. Prison isn't a playground."

"I'm not afraid of prison, or death," stated Moritz calmly. "All great revolutionists faced the danger of death. People deserve to know the truth."

They were quiet for a while.

"Look," said Moritz, "if any of you want to walk, you're free to walk. But I'm still in."

"I'm in," said Katharina. That sealed if for Johann and Emil. No way they'd let her take this on without them.

"So am I."

"Me, too."

On his way home from school one day, Emil pulled the mail out of the box. In it was a folded piece of paper with a small rose sketched in the corner.

He began to read it, then stopped, folded it and slipped it into his pocket. With a brief scan of its contents he knew he had to read it in the privacy of his own bedroom.

Then Emil ran to see Moritz.

"What's the matter?" Moritz could see excitement on Emil's face. He silenced him with a look and directed him to the shed behind his house. It was imperative that no one heard what Emil had to tell him.

"Look at this," Emil said. "It was in my mailbox. From a group that call themselves *The White Rose*."

He read aloud: *A call to all Germans!*

The war is approaching its destined end. As in the year 1918, the German government is trying to focus attention exclusively on the growing threat of submarine warfare, while in the East (Russia) the armies are constantly in retreat and invasion is imminent in the West. Mobilization in the United States has not yet reached its climax, but

119

already it exceeds anything that the world has ever seen. It has become a mathematical certainty that Hitler is leading the German people into the abyss. **Hitler cannot win the war; he can only prolong it.** *The guilt of Hitler and his minions goes beyond all measure. Retribution comes closer and closer.*

Moritz grabbed the paper from Emil's hand. "This was in your mailbox?"

"Yes."

Emil watched Moritz's face, knowing what he was reading: *But what are the German people doing? They will not see and will not listen. Blindly they follow their seducers into ruin.* Victory at any price! *is inscribed on their banner. "I will fight to the last man," says Hitler – but in the meantime the war has already been lost.*

"Wow," Moritz said.

"Do you think they know about us? Do you think this is a trap?" Suddenly Emil was suspicious of every crackling twig and stirring of the wind. He looked around nervously, certain he had been followed.

"No, I don't think it's a trap. I think it's a coincidence. Someone else is randomly distributing flyers, and happened to choose your house.

"This is great, Emil!" Moritz did a little jig. "I love it. We aren't alone. The White Rose. What a great name. We should give ourselves a name."

"This flyer wasn't handwritten, or even typed with carbon copies," Emil said. "It's duplicated. Someone has a duplicating machine."

"In Passau?"

"Doesn't seem likely. A bigger center, like Nuremberg or Munich."

It didn't matter. They just felt great that they were part of something bigger.

"We need to go out again tonight. I have flyers written from last night's broadcast."

"Maybe we should wait," Emil said. "The Gestapo will be on alert."

"But my flyer will support the message of The White Rose group. We need to blitz the town with truth. Maybe something will sink in."

"I suppose," Emil said, still unconvinced.

The four of them met in the loft, the seriousness of their mission evident in their stern expressions. They scribbled copies of the broadcast notes until their fingers cramped up. They had ten copies each, the most they'd ever written and distributed before.

They decided to split up, each covering a different section of town, and would meet in the park at St. Stephen's Cathedral when they finished.

A terrible foreboding brewed in Emil's gut, and he feared another onslaught of the trots. He slipped into an apartment block and dropped off six flyers. He considered leaving them all—that would be easiest, but it was also the most cowardly way. Their message needed to spread throughout the city.

In a common area a bulletin board littered with announcements of Nazi and community events beckoned Emil closer. He "borrowed" a tack from the Nazi rally notice and tagged his flyer to the board, watching the Nazi propaganda sheet flutter away in the evening breeze.

With three left, Emil forced himself to saunter toward the center of town, the domes of St. Stephen's guiding him. The train station was a natural spot. He saw several "black coats," SS officers, strutting purposely through town. Calm down, Emil told himself. Act natural. If he looked guilty, they would grab him for sure.

There were too many. Something was up. Emil sat on a bench watching all the people bustle by, hoping to catch the next train. He slipped the three flyers under his bottom, and waited five minutes before walking away without looking back.

What a relief to be free of those incriminating flyers! Emil felt like jogging to St. Stephen's but didn't, careful not to attract attention to himself.

Thankfully, Johann and Katharina were already there.

"Is it my imagination, or is there more activity than normal?" Emil said.

"I don't know," Johann said, shaking his head. "I think there is."

"I'm just glad to be done," said Katharina. "Moritz should be here soon."

Then they spotted him. There was no missing his awkward gait. Moritz was jogging with two Gestapo officers on his tail, guns ready. There was no way he could outrun them.

"*Halt!*"

Moritz stopped. He turned around, facing the officers. Johann, Katharina and Emil ducked behind the statue of King Maximilian Joseph, concealing themselves. A horrific tremor seized Emil. Moritz was caught! Would he give them away as well?

"You dropped this!" one officer said.

"No," Moritz said, shaking his head. "It's not mine."

The second officer stepped forward and struck Moritz across the face. Emil winced. Blood dripped from Moritz's lip.

"Don't lie! Are you a member of the White Rose?"

"I'm not."

"Yet, you are distributing treasonous materials."

"I am."

Emil couldn't believe his ears. Moritz just admitted to a crime punishable by death.

"Where are your comrades?"

"I have none. I work alone."

"Liar!" The second officer struck him again. Moritz's hand went to his face. He spit out blood.

"You are the liars!" Moritz shouted. "And Hitler is the greatest liar of them all."

Had Moritz lost his mind?

A crowd had gathered, but oddly it pushed back like a drop of water in oil.

"You dare to speak of the *Fuehrer* with such insolence?" said the first officer.

Moritz said nothing.

"The others," the second officer shouted, "where are they?"

"There are no others," Moritz said. Emil commended him for not giving them away, but he was terrified. They could *make* him talk.

Moritz blinked rapidly. In Emil's mind he saw him turn, pointing a stubby finger their way.

Then Moritz proved Emil wrong.

"You Nazi pigs!" Moritz shouted. "Hitler is a raving lunatic. Down with Hitler!" He spat in the officer's face.

The officer in turn, raised his gun. A single shot. One red dot on his forehead, and Moritz slumped to the ground.

"Moritz!" Katharina called. Johann clapped his hand over her mouth and pulled her out of sight.

Emil stared at the scene, paralyzed by shock.

Moritz had ensured that he could never talk, never betray his friends. He had died to save them.

Chapter Twenty-One

Dropping low, they sat on the bottom steps of the statue base, fear and disbelief turning their faces sheet white. They kept silent but Emil was aware of the increased movement around them, people gathering to see what had happened.

"We can't stay here like this," Emil whispered, "we look suspicious."

"We need an alibi," Johann said. "Who's at your house, Emil?"

"Just Helmut, if he's not running about. Mother's at work."

"Will he speak for us?"

Johann was asking if Helmut would lie for them. A year ago, Emil would have answered, yes, in a heartbeat, but now? He really didn't know. They barely spoke, and Helmut feared him in the same manner his parents did.

"I don't know."

"Johann." Katharina grabbed her brother's arm. "We need to separate and mingle. People we know will see us here. We are just like them witnessing a spectacle."

Emil nodded, "That's a good idea."

"Okay," Johann said, "Katharina, we're together; Emil, you're on your own. We never saw each other tonight."

Emil nodded, crawled through the shrubs in the opposite direction and merged with the crowd of onlookers. An invisible barrier kept the people back a number of meters from the scene.

Every molecule in Emil's body wanted to flee. He summoned up the courage he had just witnessed in Moritz and pressed forward through the mass of people watching. On his toes he could see the police hovering over Moritz's corpse, crumpled on the ground like dirty laundry. Emil wished he hadn't looked, but his own morbid curiosity kept him staring.

"Isn't that boy a friend of yours?"

Emil froze. It was Albert Jäger.

"No," Emil said, surprising himself.

"I thought I saw the two of you together."

"No, that wasn't me." Emil bit his lip. Tears threatened the rims of his eyes. He was glad it was getting dark.

Emil made sure that several people who knew him saw him there. They would be his alibi. Again he was questioned: Wasn't he a friend of the boy? No, Emil said, feeling like Peter who had denied knowing Jesus.

A police van pulled up and they tossed Moritz into the back. A tremendous sadness threatened to overwhelm Emil. He was sorry for Moritz, sorry for his poor mother and what this would do to her, sorry that he had lost a very good friend. When he got home, he was thankful that Helmut and Mother were out. He threw himself on his bed and cried.

The police arrived at the Radle home the next morning, with slimy Albert Jäger showing the way.

Helmut and Emil peeked around the corner as Mother opened the door. Three uniforms pushed their way into the kitchen without introduction.

"What do you want?" Mother asked, alarmed. The police said nothing, just systematically went through each room of the house, opening and searching cupboards and drawers. One officer stayed in the kitchen, one went to the living room, and the other rushed upstairs to the bedrooms.

"Officer Jäger? Please," Mother said.

Albert Jäger raised an eyebrow and kept silent. His self-righteous expression said it all; *I don't have to answer to the likes of you.*

The officer in the kitchen ran a gloved finger along the shelf of the broom closet. He paused to examine the dust on his finger before shifting his gaze to Mother.

"I, uh, work at the factory..." Mother said.

Anger boiled in Emil's gut. He was outraged at their blatant disregard for their home and their things.

The officer, who went upstairs, returned. He acknowledged his colleagues with a slight shake of his head. Of course he didn't find anything. All the evidence was at Moritz's house.

"Frau Radle?"

"Yes?"

"I must inform you that your son, Emil Radle, is required for questioning."

Helmut looked at Emil and gulped.

"What for?" said Mother.

"Your son is known to be a friend of a boy who was involved in illegal activities and all of his associates are to be questioned."

Emil stepped forward. "It's okay, Mother. I'll go."

"But, Emil..." Her hand faltered as she reached for him.

126

"I must do my duty for the *Fuehrer!*" Emil saluted to the police officer. "Officer Jäger." Even to his ears he was talking too loud. "Lead the way."

The interrogation office was small with wooden floors and two long windows looking out to dull gray skies.

Investigator Schmidt sat in a large chair on one side of a metal desk, while Emil sat opposite him, his feet flat on the floor. Investigator Schmidt lit a cigarette and blew the smoke in Emil's direction, his eyes never leaving Emil's.

"You are Emil Radle, of 45 Rosenstrasse?"

"Yes."

"Fourteen years old?"

"Yes."

"Your mother works at the clothing factory as of September, your brother is a member of the *Deutsches Jungvolk.*"

"Yes."

"Your father?"

"He's in Berlin."

Investigator Schmidt leaned forward then shuffled papers on the desk in front of him.

"Ah, yes. You were a friend of the traitor, shot dead in the street last night?"

"We were acquaintances."

"Only acquaintances? Your neighbors said they saw you with him often."

"We were in the same Hitler Youth unit, which meets regularly. And we were in the same class at school. It's natural that we would be seen together."

"Did you go to his house?"

"At times my duties with Hitler Youth required it."

"I see. Did you ever witness traitorous activities performed by the deceased?"

"No."

"Are you aware that the leaflets in question fall under the jurisdiction of special wartime law?"

"I never thought of it."

"Do you know what you get for high treason and aiding the enemy?"

Emil didn't respond. Investigator Schmidt blew more smoke in his face. "A prison sentence or death."

Again, Emil remained silent.

"He never told you about the leaflets?"

"No."

"Do you know the siblings, Johann and Katharina Ackermann?"

"Yes."

"Were you together last night?"

Did someone see them together? They had agreed to say they never saw each other.

"No."

"They were there."

"There were a lot of people out last night. I was curious about what the police were doing, like everyone else. I didn't look around, so if they were there, I didn't see them."

"I see," he said. "But you are good friends?"

"No."

"Are you sure?"

Had Johann or Katharina been interrogated already? Emil was nervous that their answers weren't lining up.

"Like Moritz, Johann and I go to the same Hitler Youth unit and are in the same class. I only know Katharina as his sister."

"So, you don't have any good friends?"

"My good friend is the *Fuehrer* only. I have no need for other close relationships except that it helps to further the good of Germany."

His career in lying, Emil thought, was firmly established.

And it seemed Emil was indeed good at it. Investigator Schmidt smiled, stubbed out his cigarette, and walked around his desk to him.

He held out his hand and Emil shook it.

"Very well, Emil Radle," he said. "I am gratified that you are a dutiful citizen. You may go."

"Thank you." Emil stood and walked towards the door.

"Herr Radle," Investigator Schmidt called.

Emil turned, "Yes, Sir?"

"We will be watching."

Moritz died on Friday, Emil was interrogated on Saturday, went to church with Mother and Helmut on Sunday, and on Monday it was back to school. But it was not business as usual.

Though cleared of any wrongdoing by Investigator Schmidt, the same was not true in the classroom. Johann and Emil were guilty by association.

"Traitor!" Friedrich hissed as Emil walked past him to his seat.

Emil tried to ignore the empty seat to his right. As Emil stared at the back of Johann's blond head in front of him, he could feel the eyes of the other students on them. They had been friends with Moritz and he had betrayed the Fatherland.

When Herr Bauer entered the room, the class quickly stood, saluting, "*Heil Hitler!*" And with more fervor than ever.

After the shuffle of twenty-five, no, twenty-four, kids re-seating themselves, an uncomfortable silence filled the classroom. Herr Bauer paced across the front of the room, ruler lightly slapping his hand.

"So, I assume everyone is aware of the hideous events that took place in our quiet town of Passau?" Herr Bauer said. "The enemy is quick and deceptive, even to masquerade as a devoted Hitler Youth member." He paused and stared pointedly at Emil and Johann. "And to sit in my classroom."

The class seemed to inhale, anticipating the lashing that was about to come.

Herr Bauer stepped down their row, stopping beside Emil's desk and tapped his ruler on the top of it. *Tap, tap, tap.*

"Emil," he said, "I understand that you had a visit with our good Investigator Schmidt."

Did he want him to answer? It was widely known.

"And you as well, Johann."

Johann answered, "Yes."

"You boys think you are clever!" Herr Bauer slapped his ruler on Johann's desk. "But be assured, the forest is now watching you."

Spinning around, he marched back to the front of the class. "A traitor in my classroom!" he shouted. "A shame and a disgrace!"

Like Hitler, shouting first then whispering, he lowered his voice. "It has recently come to my attention that the traitor, whose name we are now forbidden to speak, had Jewish blood. This was a well kept secret, and explains why he went crazy all of a sudden."

Emil knew for certain that Moritz was not even a tiny bit Jewish. Herr Bauer had made that up.

"A treasonous pig! He should have been hung by the neck for all to see, dead already or not!"

The back of Johann's neck turned red, and he twitched in his seat. Emil had a bad feeling.

Johann burst out, "He was not..."

Suddenly Emil was on his feet, interrupting, "...not worthy of our time and attention. He was a pig and a traitor to our great *Fuehrer* and Fatherland, a menace to society and our good fellow German citizens and an obstacle to our quest for *Lebensraum*!" Emil felt like he was having an out of body experience. He slid back into his seat, but not before seeing the fury in Johann's eyes.

Herr Bauer hardly held back his surprise at the outburst.

"Thank you, Emil," he said, his lips widening into a crooked grin. "Well said."

He returned to his desk. Unfortunately, the current excitement didn't thwart his intention to give them a math lesson.

He read out loud: "A mentally handicapped person costs the public four Reichmarks a day, a cripple five and a half Reichmarks and a convicted criminal eight and a half Reichmarks. Cautious estimates state that within the bound of the German Reich, three hundred thousand persons are being cared for in Public mental institutions.

"How many marriage loans at one thousand Reichmarks per couple could be financed annually from the funds allocated to the institutions?"

Emil caught up to Johann on the path through a field Johann used as a short cut from school to his house.

"Johann, wait up!"

Johann turned and jumped on him. They landed with a thump, the wind knocked out of Emil.

"You traitor!" Johann spat.

"I'm not," Emil squeaked out. They rolled in the dirt, dust filling their eyes. Johann's bony elbows dug into Emil's ribs. "Get off of me."

"I don't know what side you're on, Emil."

"I'm on your side," Emil said, breathless. Johann was bigger and heavier, but Emil was strong, too. He pushed back. They rolled the other way; broken grass stalks cut Emil's skin.

"You're playing both sides."

"What do you think would have happened to you, if you came to Moritz's defense?"

They rolled again and Emil found himself face down, Johann on his back.

"Johann, I had to..."

Johann pushed Emil's face into the ground. Something warm oozed down his face.

"Ouch, my nose is bleeding!"

Johann rolled off Emil, onto his back. His breath came out in heavy pants. "He was our friend."

"He did what he did to save us," Emil said, breathing hard. "I did what I did to save you."

They lay flat on their backs, staring at the bright blue sky. A hawk circled overhead then dove into the field; they heard the screech of some small animal, a rabbit or rat, now in the death grip of the bird's claws. A cool breeze brushed over their skin, drying their sweat. It seemed like just another quiet autumn day in 1942, no sign of the war that was waging over Europe.

"I'm sorry, Emil," Johann said. "I just miss him so much."

"I do too, Johann."

Johann got up first and held out his hand. Emil took it. "Friends again?" he said.

Emil nodded. "Friends still."

Chapter Twenty-Two

"Heinz has been drafted!" Emil fought for breath after jogging to the Ackerman farm with the news.

"What?" Johann said, though he'd heard Emil clearly. "Oh, man. It's starting." He slumped into a cool kitchen chair and drew his hand through his hair.

Katharina entered the small kitchen and leaned against the door frame. "What's the matter?"

"It's Heinz," Emil said. "He's been drafted."

"Oh."

"His parents are hosting a big party." Emil swallowed before adding, "Irmgard invited me to go."

Katharina stared hard at him. "Are you going?"

Emil stared back. "I don't think I have a choice."

"You don't, Emil," Johann said. "In fact, you shouldn't even be here. It's not good for people to see us together so soon after...."

"I know. I just had to tell you about Heinz." And, Emil thought to himself. He missed his friends. He missed Katharina.

Emil left before they could get started talking about other news, like the fact that the German army had attacked Stalingrad in Russia and now occupied the city. Many Germans didn't know if they should rejoice or mourn.

Hadn't Germany signed a non-aggression pact with Stalin? Wasn't Poland a shared victory? Surely, they wouldn't take this invasion lying down. The Russian army was notorious for their brutality. People were nervous. Emil was nervous.

Herr and Frau Schultz hosted the party in their home. The Schultzes were like a movie family: Mother and Father, Heinz, Rolf and Imrgard, all tall, blond, blue-eyed and beautiful.

Frau Schultz was the perfect hostess, smiling warmly as their guests arrived, taking their jackets and hanging them in the wardrobe. For some reason Frau Schultz didn't have to work outside the home like Emil's mother did. And she wore a nice dress, almost new. Maybe it was because Herr Schultz was a commander in the Nazi Party. Rumors flew that he actually had meetings with the *Fuehrer* himself.

"As our great leader has said," Herr Schultz said loudly to his guests, "Once we are masters in Europe, then we will enjoy the dominant position in the world!"

Where once Emil had worried that the Germans might not win the war, now he worried that it might be possible. Herr Bauer had boasted recently about how the Germans were now in command of a landmass larger than America, and that Greater Germany was now more densely populated and more economically productive than anywhere in the world. The latest new map of Germany showed her expanding west to east from France to the Black Sea, and from Norway in the north all the way south to the Sahara in Africa. That meant Germany occupied almost one-third of Europe and ruled nearly half its population.

"Hi, Emil," Irmgard sat next to him, an open beer bottle in her hand. Her eyes were glassy, her breath stale. "I'm so glad you could make it!"

Emil nodded in response. "Thanks for inviting me."

"Isn't this exciting! Heinz is a man now. I can't believe he's joining the army."

"Yeah, it's great." Emil said with enthusiasm he didn't feel. "I wish I could go with him."

"Oh, some day you will, Emil," Irmgard gushed. "Someday it will be your turn to make the Fatherland proud." Emil once believed this would all be over before he was old enough to enlist. Now he wasn't so sure.

"Where is Johann Ackerman?"

Emil shrugged. "Why should I know?"

"Oh, no reason. I thought you two chummed around together."

Emil paused thoughtfully, staring at the large bright red Nazi flag with the black swastika in the middle hanging on the wall. Was she trying to trap him? He finally responded, "Only when it serves the Fatherland."

"That's what I like about you, Emil."

"What?"

"Besides your charming good looks?" she did that weird thing with her eyelashes, flapping them like she had dust in her eye. "You love the Fatherland more than your own life."

Friedrich and Wolfgang entered the room, saving Emil from further awkward scrutiny.

"Oh, Friedrich, Wolfgang!" Irmgard cried leaving Emil's side and rushing to give each of them a hug. "I'm so glad you boys could come to help us celebrate!"

"We wouldn't miss it for the world." Friedrich and Wolfgang circled the room, shaking everyone's hand. *"Guten Abend, alle zusammen!"* Good evening, everyone. Then Rolf gave them beer and they joined the older boys, listening to Heinz talk about the army and what a privilege it was to join.

After a few rounds of beer, they began to sing Hitler Youth songs, swinging full mugs through the air, *Today Germany is ours and tomorrow the whole world...*

Emil decided it was time to slip out the back.

On a bland November day, Heinz left for the Russian front. The whole Hitler Youth unit went to the train station to see him off. So did Irmgard's League for German Girls.

"Heinz, you look so handsome in your uniform!" Irmgard said. He'd been issued the standard army uniform; this one looked faded and worn, like it'd had a previous owner, some poor soul who didn't make it. *Kind of eerie,* Emil thought. He recalled the early days of their Hitler Youth meetings when Emil wanted nothing more than to be just like Heinz Schultz.

Now he pitied him.

"Will you write to me, Heinz?" Elsbeth gushed. All the girls swooned, dreamy eyed. Johann was right about girls and love.

Rolf slapped his brother on the back. "You give'em hell, brother, and come back to tell us about it."

Heinz laughed with confidence. "I'll return. The Reds have nothing on me."

Emil shoved his hands in his pockets and shimmied around a bit to keep warm. Johann was doing the same. They didn't say much. They didn't care if Heinz left or stayed. It was cold and Emil wanted to go home, that was all he cared about.

Finally the trained arrived, and they all took turns shaking Heinz's hand.

"Good, luck," Emil said.

His mother shed one lone tear. "I'm so proud of you, son."

Heinz waved from the window of the train, as it slowly chugged off.

"I'm in love with your brother, Irmgard," said Elsbeth. "Maybe, when he gets back, he'll ask me to marry him?"

Irmgard didn't answer her question. "I bet he'll kill hundreds of Soviets," she said instead. "He's such a great soldier!"

Chapter Twenty-Three

Everyone tried to ignore the fact that thousands were dying on the eastern front every day, including thousands of Germans. The German propaganda machine could no longer hide such staggering numbers to fool the people. Passau's own number of war dead grew, and funerals were a daily occurrence.

Because of this crisis in the east, the Hitler Youth were instructed to begin a mass Winter Help campaign to collect metals, clothing, skis, anything to help the war effort.

Emil took Helmut out to canvass their neighborhood every day after school.

"Thank you, Frau Schneider," Emil said, as she quickly tossed a small tin pot to them and closed the door. Winter had hit hard and Emil and Helmut jumped up and down to keep warm.

"Let's skip the next one," Helmut said, "I'm freezing."

The rebel in Emil wanted to say *Yes, let's skip some houses*; but the part of him that played the fanatic knew he could not.

"Not yet," Emil said. They continued house-to-house, collecting spoons, clothes, tools. The people knew they would come again the next day and so were rationing their "donations," instead of giving them everything at once.

They wouldn't dare say it, but the German housewives were running out of supplies for their own families.

Herr Franke came to the door of the next house. He handed Emil a hammer. "That's my last tool, boys," he said grimly. He reminded Emil of an older version of his father—his worried eyes, his frown.

Emil and Helmut dragged their loot behind them; it was too heavy to lift off the ground.

"Has Mother heard anything of Father?" Emil asked.

"No. She checks the post every day, but hasn't received a letter in weeks."

"Oh."

"I'm worried, Emil. So many are dying."

"He'll be okay."

"How do you know?"

"I don't know. But Mother prays."

Emil was shivering, and didn't want to talk about Father any more. Besides, something across the street distracted him. It was Katharina with a group of girls from her League. Helmut saw him looking at her.

"Do you like her?" Helmut asked, smiling.

"No!" Emil said, too quickly.

"Yes you do! I can tell."

"That's Johann's sister. It would be the same as liking my own sister."

"I think you like her. Your cheeks are red!"

"My cheeks are red because it's freezing cold out, you moron!" Emil pushed Helmut into the snow bank. He glanced over at Katharina. She saw everything, but she didn't wave or smile. She acted like she didn't even know Emil. Good for her.

Helmut stood and brushed the snow off his trousers.

"Emil, I'm freezing, let's skip some houses."

Emil was freezing, too. "Okay, just this once, because it's so cold."

They canvassed every other house on the way home, but unfortunately, Rolf witnessed their transgression.

"*Heil Hitler!*" he said. He wore his winter uniform proudly, though even his zeal couldn't mask the chill he was fighting.

"*Heil Hitler!*"

"You must dress warmer," Rolf said. "You were skipping houses."

"Our bags are almost full," Emil said. "We were headed to the synagogue to drop them off."

"You must go back to the homes you missed."

"We will. Right away."

"Continue, then."

"Yes, of course."

Rolf clicked the heels of his boots, and saluted.

"*Heil Hitler.*"

"*Heil Hitler,*" Emil and Helmut responded. When Rolf was out of sight, Helmut clicked his heels in imitation, tightening his face the way Rolf did.

Emil didn't know if Helmut momentarily forgot that he was there or if he still trusted him a little bit, but he couldn't help but laugh. Helmut's face flushed with relief and he started to laugh, too. No matter what the war had done to them, they were still brothers.

They ignored Rolf's orders and dragged their heavy bags to the synagogue.

Chapter Twenty-Four

Grandmother Heinrich had had a collection of soft lines around her eyes and mouth; it seemed she had always been smiling. At least this was how Emil's mother described her. But Mother never mentioned that Grandmother Heinrich had a sister, until Great Tante Gerta showed up at the door one day, unannounced.

Mother was unable to hide her surprise, and barely her dismay. But as always, her manners were impeccable.

"Tante Gerta! Please come in."

"*Heil Hitler!*" she responded, stepping purposefully through the door. Emil and Helmut glanced at each other, their eyebrows furrowing together.

"I have been re-assigned to work at the prison for women. It is not far from here and since your husband is currently away, I can be of assistance to you."

A shadow of fear crossed Mother's face. Emil could see why Mother had never mentioned her. Tante Gerta was tall, with bony shoulders, but unlike other tall women who slouched to hide their height, she stood rigid. She had a tight bun of dirty-blonde hair, piercing Aryan-blue eyes and thin lips that moved in silence as she scrutinized them.

Emil was afraid, too.

Tante Gerta dropped a medium sized suitcase on the kitchen floor and began an impromptu inspection. Mother

142

was mortified as Tante Gerta opened a kitchen cupboard and ran a white-gloved finger along the inside.

"Tante Gerta!" Mother could keep quiet no longer.

"Cleanliness is next to godliness, Leni," she said in clipped flawless German. "And I'm doing you a favor. I happen to know that the SS will be doing rounds in this neighborhood next week."

"To check for dust?" my mother said, incredulous.

"Precisely. A German wife and mother must keep her home clean, for the sake of her family and for the pride of the Fatherland."

Tante Gerta picked up her suitcase. "Please, where shall I retire?"

"Helmut," Mother said. "Move your things in with Emil. Emil, take Tante Gerta's suitcase upstairs for her."

Helmut scurried off, with Emil hauling Tante Gerta's heavy suitcase right behind him.

Later, while Tante Gerta was "settling in," Mother pulled a folded piece of paper from her apron pocket.

"What's that?" Emil said.

"It's a 'request' that every household send one person to attend a weekly Nazi party meeting."

Emil couldn't imagine Mother stepping foot in one of those.

"I wondered what we would do, Emil, and... I didn't want to send you." She smiled softly and nodded toward the stairs. "She's an answer to prayer."

"Oh." Emil understood. "Tante Gerta can go, now."

"Yes, Tante Gerta can go."

Having Tante Gerta in the house was like living with a vicious guard dog that growled in its throat through bared teeth. The Radle family trod carefully around her, fearful of

143

the painful bite that came in the form of a harsh verbal lashing. Thankfully, she didn't spend a lot of time at home.

One afternoon there was a knock on the door.

"Johann?"

"Are you alone, Emil?" he whispered. His face was flush with excitement, and he clearly had news.

"Yes."

"I found this." Johann handed Emil a folded piece of paper. He opened it carefully. It was damp and most of the printing was smudged, especially on one side, but he could still make some of it out.

"Another pamphlet from The White Rose," Emil whispered.

"I found it on the floor in the lobby of my Onkel's apartment."

Fellow fighters in the Resistance!

Shaken and broken, our people behold the loss of the men of Stalingrad. Three hundred and thirty thousand German men have been senselessly and irresponsibly driven to death and destruction by the inspired strategy of our World War I Private First Class. We have the Fuehrer *to thank.*

"Three hundred and thirty thousand?" Emil said. Unbelievable. "With so many men lost, how can we hold the front?"

"Maybe we can't."

Will we continue to sacrifice the rest of our German youth to the base ambitions of a Party clique? No, never! The day of reckoning has come....

In the name of German youth we demand restitution by Adolf Hitler's state of our personal freedom, the most precious treasure that we have, out of which he has swindled us in the most miserable way.

"This is good," Emil said.

"I know."

We grew up in a state where all free expression of opinion is unscrupulously suppressed. The Hitler Youth, the SA, the SS have all tried to drug us, to revolutionize us, to regiment us in the most promising young years of our lives....

Freedom and honor! For ten long years Hitler and his coadjutors have manhandled, squeezed, twisted and debased these two splendid German words to the point of nausea...

The frightful bloodbath has opened the eyes of even the stupidest German—it is a slaughter that they arranged in the name of "freedom and honor of the German nation"...

Students!

That was all Emil could make out.

"Students? The White Rose must be a group of students at a University."

"Munich or Nuremberg?" Johann said.

"Could be anywhere. What do you think we should do?"

"We can copy this and then distribute."

"I don't know, Johann. Moritz..."

"It's for Moritz that we have to do this. If we don't keep resisting, his death is for nothing."

Emil let out a long breath. "Okay. When?"

"The Loft. Today."

Emil arrived first. The farm was like a ghost town, only a few cows left, from what was once a thriving milk farm. The Nazis had taken everything.

Emil sneaked in through the back door of the barn, and patted a cow on the head as he passed by. He climbed up the wooden planks that worked as a ladder to the loft and fell into the hay. There was a small window on the south side, so there was enough light to do what he and Johann had planned to do. A low wooden bench rested against one wall. Emil went to it, hunched over because of the low ceiling, and sat down.

Soon, he heard the door open, a soft whisper to the cow and the creaking of the ladder. Johann's blond head bobbed into sight.

And then, Katharina's.

"Why did you bring her?" Emil said feeling angry.

"Because she's an extra writer."

Katharina climbed over to the bench and sat down. "Quit talking about me like I'm not here."

"It's more dangerous now than before." Emil didn't want the same thing that happened to Moritz to happen to Katharina.

"I know that. And I'm staying."

Once again Emil was out-numbered. "Fine," he conceded. "Let's get going."

Johann opened his jacket and reached back to an open seam. He slowly pulled out the leaflet. Katharina opened her bag and pulled out paper and pens. They used the bench as a table and started writing.

Chapter Twenty-Five

1943
FEBRUARY

"Let's go to the movies tonight," Emil said. "We need to get our minds off the war."

"I don't know if I can stomach the garbage they call movies." Johann referred to all the Nazi propaganda in the German Films. "However, if we first meet at the loft?" He wanted to transcribe more leaflets, to continue spreading the message of the White Rose. Emil nodded and they set a time.

The film was called *I Accuse*–a story of a physician whose suffering wife persuades him to poison her. During the courtroom drama, Emil slipped the leaflets out of his pocket and shoved them under his bottom. Johann and Katharina, who had taken seats in other sections of the theater, did the same. Afterwards, they walked home together.

"Funny how all the talented and handsome actors presented the arguments for the doctor to kill his wife,"

Katharina said. "And all the annoying ones wanted to save her."

"Well, you've heard the rumors?" Emil said.

"Yes," Johann said. "Apparently the mentally ill are being forced admittance into certain hospitals, where they always die of some mysterious illness."

"And the bodies are cremated before the families can see them," Katharina added.

"Do you think it's true?" Emil asked. He found the whole concept unbelievable.

"I hope not," said Katharina. "But then, they *are* making movies like *I Accuse*."

They made their way down the cobble streets towards home when a man in a ragged brown jacket turned the corner shouting, "*Stalingrad has fallen! Stalingrad has fallen!*"

"No," Katharina gasped. "Can it be true?"

They rushed back to Emil's house to hear reports on the state radio that the Soviets had indeed won back their city. The Germans had been defeated once again and there wasn't enough propaganda that could hide this fact.

"It's happening, just like *the* radio said," Johann said stiffly.

"This means they were right about Germany losing horribly on the Eastern front," Emil said. Now the worst had happened. Germany's army had surrendered and for the first time Germans dared to doubt. The *Fuehrer* was wrong, we could lose the war.

One-sheet newspaper extras sold on the street the next day. The people were called to a national period of mourning.

Then on February 18, 1943, the minister of propaganda, Dr. Josef Goebbels gave a speech in the *Sportpalast* in Berlin. The whole school was called to an assembly to hear it on the radio.

Emil sat on the bleachers warmed by the energy in the room. The speakers crackled and hummed, then suddenly, the noise of thousands of soldiers and civilians cheering in the background while Goebbels' authoritative voice declared Germany's resolve to bring a glorious victory.

"Do you want total war?" he bellowed. Emil's spine tingled with apprehension. "Do you want, if necessary, a war more total and radical than we could possibly imagine today?"

A thick lump formed in Emil's throat. Did they really still believe they could win this war? Had they learned nothing of the Stalingrad tragedy?

"Yes, yes, yes!" The cheers of the crowd in Berlin were deafening, even through the school speakers. Then like those possessed, the teachers joined in, followed by the students, "Yes, yes, yes!" Tears of joy ran down their faces.

There were tears on Emil's face, too, but his were of fear and sorrow. And great disappointment.

On the same day they learned the location of The White Rose group. Munich University. On February 18, 1943, the papers reported the news. Three students in their early twenties were arrested. Brother and sister, Hans and Sophie Scholl and Christoph Probst. Hans and Christoph were medical students and Sophie studied biology and philosophy. And now they were prisoners of the Third Reich.

Then, only a short four days later, they were beheaded.

Emil, Katharina and Johann met in the loft when they heard the news. Katharina curled up and cried softly into her knees.

"We can't keep going," Emil said.

"Do you really think we should stop now?" said Johann

Katharina wiped her face with her sleeve. "If they got caught, and the Huebner Group got caught, what makes you think that we won't get caught, too?"

Johann persisted, "But is quitting the answer?"

"What good did it do them? What good did it do Germany?" Emil countered. "Nothing, nothing at all."

They were defeated. The death of the White Rose meant the death of their mission, too. Their resistance to National Socialism through flyer distribution was over.

Chapter Twenty-Six

einz Schultz died in Russia.

The whole school went to his funeral. It was only thirty minutes long, because there were so many funeral services performed every day.

A Nazi ceremony was performed at the Town Hall. A large portrait of Hitler hung on the wall above the plain wooden casket. An SS officer said a few words, but Emil couldn't hear him over the wailing of Irmgard and her mother.

It was the first time someone in their own circle had died fighting Hitler's war. Moritz's death was different. No one here, besides Emil, Johann, and Katharina, would ever call Moritz a hero.

The mood matched the weather, dark and brooding. Germany's dying youth in the abstract was somehow palatable, an honorable sacrifice for the greater good. Not so when it was one of your own. Herr Schultz made no effort to comfort his wife and daughter. His own stoic face was carefully controlled.

Rolf stood resolute, and then made his way to the front to speak.

"Heinz was the finest specimen of the master race that could be found in the Reich. He was disciplined, strong and

151

fearless. He loved his *Fuehrer* above all and proudly gave his life for the Fatherland."

Rolf, tall and lean, stood earnestly in his Hitler Youth uniform. Emil couldn't help but notice how worn and patched up it was. Much like his. Much like everyone's.

"We must not let our loss be wasted with defeat!" he shouted, breaking the solemn quiet. "Heinz's death must count for something, will count for something. He was an inspiration to us all, not to back down when things get hard, but to get up and to keep going. I, for one, will not lie down. I beseech you to stand with me."

Herr Schultz started with light clapping of his hands. Others joined in until it was a raucous applause with everyone on their feet, hardly a dry eye in the place. Elsbeth applauded with special enthusiasm. "I'll never forget you, Heinz," she shouted.

Herr Bauer gave his students the rest of the day off.

"Before Moritz, I never saw a person die," Johann said. They were heading back to the barn.

"I didn't like Heinz," Emil said, "but I didn't wish to see him dead, either."

"Now it seems like death is everywhere," Johann said. "How long before it's us, Emil?"

"What can happen to us? We're too young to go to the front; the bombers are attacking big cities in the west. We'll be okay."

"You know, Emil, I love Germany. I really do."

"Of course," Emil said. "So do I."

Johann studied him. "But will you die for it?"

"If I have to, but..."

"I think you're wrong. We will have to fight. And when they call me, I'm not going to go."

Emil swallowed hard. "But you love Germany."

"Yes," Johann said, glancing over his shoulder and lowering his voice so Emil could barely hear him. "But I despise its leader."

Emil didn't say anything. Would he fight in the war if called? He still hoped it wouldn't come to that.

Chapter Twenty-Seven

"We will yet win this war!" Tante Gerta proclaimed. She was still rejoicing over Goebbel's declaration of Total War.

Mother scrubbed potatoes at the sink, her back turned to Tante Gerta. Emil set the table for three, thankful that Tante Gerta always caught the 12:00 bus.

"It would be nice to eat something other than potatoes," was all Mother said.

"At least you have plenty of those, and you should be thankful," Tante Gerta scolded. Her good humor was over. And Emil was sure she got more than potatoes at her work, being the faithful Nazi that she was. She certainly hadn't lost weight like the rest of Passau. Mother, in comparison, was a rail, her eyes sunken with dark circles.

"Oh, I am thankful, Tante Gerta," she said. "Just saying, it would be nice." Tante Gerta left for work in a huff. "And a bit of butter to fry them too, right, Emil? Wouldn't that be nice?" Mother cast Emil a sly grin.

"Yes, Mother, it would," Emil said. Then, to his surprise, she pulled out a scrap of material from her pocket and emptied a plop of butter from it, into the pan. Emil's eyes widened, and a big smile spread across his face. The smell of potatoes fried in actual butter was intoxicating.

"Where did you get that?" he said.

154

Again, a sly grin. "You might notice that our teapot is gone."

"You traded Grandmother Heinrich's silver teapot for a spot of butter?" Emil didn't know if he was happy or dismayed.

"There's no tea anyway," she said. "Besides, it's your brother's birthday. Go call him for supper."

As always, they bowed their heads while Mother prayed over the food. With the addition of butter, Emil and Helmut added a hearty "Amen."

"Happy Birthday, Helmut," Emil said, rubbing the boy's head. "I'm sorry I don't have a present."

"That's okay," Helmut said. "Butter is the best gift anyway."

The next day a Hitler Youth leader and Herr Jäger, the official SS block commander, showed up at their door asking for Helmut. They didn't waste any time, Emil thought.

Mother resisted. "What is the hurry? The boy only just turned ten yesterday."

"Frau Radle," the Hitler Youth leader, no older than Emil, replied. "Your son is only on loan to you. He belongs to Hitler, as do all of Germany's youth."

It angered Emil that this boy was so disrespectful to his mother.

Herr Jäger nodded in agreement. As the head of surveillance in their neighborhood his job was to manage the tongues of the Nazi faithful. As such, he found it his duty to pry. Anything the people said or did was subject to scrutiny and possible prosecution. It was rumored now that they had one spy for every forty people. That was why

155

German folk now had a habit of looking over their shoulders.

"Your son," the Hitler Youth leader said.

"It's all right, Mother," Helmut said, his eyes wide. "You know I'm all right." To Emil, it sounded like a secret code. Helmut was reassuring Mother that he wasn't about to fall for the lies he would be bombarded with.

Like they thought Emil had.

Helmut embraced Mother quickly and left with the officers.

"He's a good boy." Mother wiped away a tear. "A very good boy."

Chapter Twenty-Eight

Their losses in Stalingrad along with all the losses on the eastern and western fronts led to a severe shortage of soldiers. News came of a new call to arms.

It seemed Emil and Johann had escaped front line duty, but they weren't to expect a vacation. All children aged ten to fifteen were enlisted into the war effort. The younger boys and the girls would work on farms with food production and the older boys would run the Flak guns or help in the fields. That meant no more school. Their excitement about not having to deal with Herr Bauer anymore was short lived, as the students found out that long hours in the fields was a fate worse than half that time in the classroom.

For Emil it meant going to the flight school in Nuremberg where he was to train as a pilot when not manning the Flak.

He couldn't believe he was actually going to attend flight school! Not glider camp, like last time, but actual flight school. Real airplanes—this was his dream. Despite everything, the war and all the troubles that came with it, he still longed to fly, and he decided to ignore the fact that they were calling him at nearly fifteen years of age because of massive pilot losses.

157

"We just missed being called into action," Johann said grimly.

"Yeah?"

"So, what happens this summer, when we turn sixteen?"

"Maybe the war will be over by then."

"Emil," Johann said, shaking his head. "Sometimes you are very naive."

He could be right about that, Emil thought.

He was visiting Johann's farm, helping to plant the potato patch that most of the neighborhood got their potatoes from. The soil was dark, and as Emil attacked it with his hoe, the sweet earthy scent blended with the warmth of the morning sun to comfort and distract him. He didn't even see her coming.

"Hello, Emil"

"Katharina?" His heart skipped a beat. "Hello."

She smiled shyly and started hoeing the row opposite Emil. He found himself staring.

He recalled their "race" through the city square last winter and how, for him anyway, things between them had changed. He thought about her a lot. More than a lot, all the time. He stole glances at her when they had met at the loft, careful not to get caught by Johann, all the while pushing down those prickly growing feelings he couldn't name, telling himself she was just one of the boys—nothing more. This war had made him an expert at pretending to be something he was not.

Over the last year, Katharina had morphed into a woman. Gone was the bony shouldered, flat-chested young girl he'd first met. Even with the current government imposed famine, she was soft and curvy. Every time Emil saw her he felt like he was seeing her for the first time.

"I'm going to miss you," she said, surprising him.

"What?"

"I'm going to miss you when you go to Nuremberg."

"Really?"

Now *she* was staring. *What did she see when she looked at him?* Emil was suddenly self-conscious. He was tall, and lean like all German boys and he was strong and athletic, the muscles in his arms and thighs all larger than the year before. He had started wearing his father's shirts recently due to his shoulders getting broader, and using Father's razors on his face. For the first time, Emil wondered if he was handsome.

Emil thought maybe Katharina was thinking that he was.

She cleared her throat. "I hope you will be okay there." She didn't go back to hoeing, just stood there watching him. She was only one row away, one large step. Emil swallowed.

"I'm just training at the flight school. It will be quite a while before I actually fly."

"Will you write to me?"

Katharina wanted him to write to her. A burst of warmth exploded in his chest. "Sure," he said, feeling a smile spread across his face.

She smiled back and returned to work. Emil experienced a strange emotion, then. He thought it might be happiness. Something he hadn't felt in a very long time.

Chapter Twenty-Nine

They really shouldn't have been starving in Passau. The farmlands were not bombed out like in many other communities, yet, even with all the youth sent to help the farmers, they still had a shortage of food. This was partly due to crop loss as a result of an early frost, but it was also due to the fact that they were losing the war. All the nation's supplies were being sent to support the war effort, so not only were the clothing and shoe factories not tending to the civilians, neither were the food trucks.

Families were given food-rationing coupons, but the stores were empty. Most of what they grew in Passau got shipped off to the soldiers in the east. All the train cars were used to take coal to the fronts as well, and there weren't enough left to ship coal to the outlining communities. So in addition to being hungry, the people froze, too.

Hunger can make a person very irritable, Emil thought. Especially at the dinner table when all they had to eat was boiled potatoes, skins on. No butter anymore. And Mother still insisted on giving thanks.

"Dear Heavenly Father," she prayed. "Thank you for this food. Please keep Peter safe and bring him home soon. Amen."

"Mother," Emil said, exasperated. "How can you keep praying and giving thanks? All we've eaten for weeks now are potatoes."

"Emil, there are many people pulled into this ungodly war who are suffering much more than you. Be grateful."

"I'm sorry, Mother." Emil lowered his head and spooned in a dry mouthful of mashed potato.

"It's okay. This war has changed us all."

"I wish Father would come home," Helmut said. Emil could see his brother's jaw working to create enough saliva to wet the mush in his mouth so he could force it down. Helmut pinched his eyes together, and Emil understood the pain and fear he was fighting. He admired his little brother for putting on a brave front. He was just a kid.

Maybe God did hear Mother's prayers, because the next day Father came home. It was late in the evening. Mother had returned from a sixteen-hour shift at the factory, and Emil and Helmut had returned home from their shift in the fields, the same field where Emil would continue to work until he left for Nuremberg.

Emil was lighting the fireplace when he heard the front door open. He turned around and there he was. Without thinking twice; he was in Father's arms, along with Helmut and Mother.

"Peter, oh, Peter!" Mother cried. They pressed into him so hard that he almost lost his balance.

"Whoa," he said, laughing. "I've survived war duty just to be mauled to death by my own family!"

They gathered around the fire, the first time in fourteen months, as a complete family. Father looked worn and thin, but not as bad as some of the soldiers Emil had seen in town on leave. This was because Father worked in the offices of the war administration and not actually on the front lines.

"How long are you home, Father?" Emil asked.

"Only a week, son."

Emil saw mother wince at that. They'd all hoped it would be longer.

"And," Father sighed, "I'm not being re-assigned to my desk."

"What do you mean?" said Mother.

"Things are not going well on the Eastern front. I don't know what you've heard, but the casualties have been immense. I'm to join the army."

"Oh, no," Mother whispered. Her eyes welled up, but she swallowed hard, determined to stay strong.

"Who will take your job, then, Father?" Helmut asked.

"A capable older gentleman. He's been pulled out of retirement to serve the Reich."

Just a twinge of bitterness when he said "Reich". Emil remembered how adamantly he'd been against Hitler and Nazism.

"I think it's time for bed," Mother said. "Peter, you must be exhausted."

"No more than all of you. I'm so sorry you have to work so hard."

"At least you're home," Mother said. "At least you're home for now."

Father was home on leave, and so, as long as he wore his uniform, no one could accuse him of being lazy just because he and Emil sat on a park bench overlooking the Danube River.

The sun poked through gray haze, long, spiky rays that bounced off the water.

"Beautiful," Father said. "God is still in control of the weather."

Meaning Hitler wasn't.

"Father," Emil said. There was so much he wanted to tell him, so much he needed him to know.

"Yes, Emil?"

"I, um," Emil couldn't help but steal glances, watching for others around them. No one must hear what he said, but this could be his only chance to tell Father. To confess.

He leaned into his father, laying his head on his shoulder. It was an uncustomary act of closeness between them, but Emil did it more out of a sense of protection.

"I'm not, you know," he couldn't quite say it out loud. *Nazi*. "Moritz, when he died, he wasn't alone."

"No?"

"I was there. We did it, all of it, together." Emil didn't think it necessary to bring Johann and Katharina into this. It was his confession to his father, not theirs.

"I see."

"So, you and me, we're the same in a way. We're fighting on the outside, but not the inside."

Emil sat up and looked into his father's eyes. Did he understand what he'd just said? Really understand?

Father nodded slowly, his eyes filling with emotion. Relief? Pride? A smile tugged at Father's lips. "I'm happy to hear that, son."

Emil smiled back. Sharing his burden with Father had lifted the guilt he'd felt from lying to him, to everyone, about Moritz's death that day. Some of it, anyway. Emil could breathe again.

In a blink, Father was gone. They took the bus together to the train station, all bravely waiting for the whistle to blow. Emil had flashbacks of the younger, well-dressed,

163

plumper family they once were. Now Mother and Father seemed old to him; shoulders stooped over, burdens so heavy to carry. This version of his family wore clothes with fabric too thin and repeatedly patched over and shoes scuffed with holes breaking through. Even Father in his "new" uniform was poorly dressed.

They were all thinking the same thing. Would they see him again? Dead or alive? If he died, the chances were great they would not. The war deceased were no longer shipped home for family burials but simply buried where they fell.

The warning whistle blew. Father hugged Helmut first.

"Be strong, Helmut. Help your mother."

"Yes, Father." Helmut wiped a stray tear, turning so we wouldn't see him cry.

"Emil, you are a man now. I want you to know I am proud of you. Please be careful in Nuremberg."

Emil's eyes burned. His throat tightened. "Yes, Father," he could hardly speak. "Thank you."

He was proud of him?

The last whistle blew and Mother cried unashamedly. Emil turned away as they kissed good-bye. He wanted to give them their privacy and quite frankly, it was embarrassing.

Father boarded the train and sat by a window, stretching his arm out to them. *Good-bye, Father.*

The train inched forward and Emil, Helmut and Mother, with a sea of other people saying good bye to their loved ones, ran after it.

"I love you, Peter!" Mother shouted. "God be with you."

Yes, Emil thought, *please God, be with him.*

Chapter Thirty

Kaiserburg Imperial Castle was perched on a low hill, and overlooked the plains that embraced Nuremberg, watching over the city like royalty. An ancient stone fence surrounded the well-populated, old-town center which was divided into two sections by the river Pegnitz.

The air force base sat on the northern outskirts in the middle of farmland. It included a row of one-storey bunkhouses, a larger structure with a dining hall and a meeting room where the newly inducted met for classes. Four Flak stations situated to the south and east of the bunkhouse were close enough the youth could reach them in minutes. The guns—massive, leaning canons— much bigger than the single-man ones Emil had trained on in Passau, were each surrounded by a wood and concrete wall as tall as a man. A vegetable garden grew immediately south of the guns. Guns and gardens. Not a natural pairing like salt and pepper, but Emil hoped it meant they would eat regularly.

When Emil arrived at his room, a blond, blue-eyed youth was already there, unpacking.

"You're my bunkmate?" the boy asked him.

"Looks like it."

"Name's Georg." He held out his hand. "Georg Stramm. From Regensberg."

"I'm Emil Radle. From Passau."

"I hope you don't mind, I took the top bunk."

"Not at all," Emil said.

"You fly?"

"Not yet. That's why I'm here, though." Emil unbuckled his suitcase and mimicked Georg, putting clothing in the bottom drawer of the dresser, and hung his jacket on a hook.

"Me, too. I'm eager to spread my wings," Georg spread out his arms in demonstration. "And take on those nasty Reds."

The Red Army. After Stalingrad, the words put fear into Emil's heart. The Reich tried to keep the truth from getting out. They didn't want the common person to know about the terror and torture. But word got around. It was hard to keep that kind of thing a secret.

There was a bell, kind of like school, and all the new recruits were rounded up and split into three groups. Emil and Georg ended up in the same group, led by SS Officer Spiegl, a tall, bulky no-nonsense looking man.

He took them on a tour of the city. Seven youth piled into the back of an army vehicle.

They drove passed the double steeples of St. Sebaldus Church, along the front side of the block-long four-storey brick and stone City Hall.

They had just crossed one of the many stone bridges over the Pegnitz when the alarms went off.

Emil spotted dark flecks in the sky.

Allied planes. Dropping bombs.

Emil stared, mouth open wide as the Flak towers on the west side of the city started shooting into the sky. Bright orange streaks of light. And then one hit! The target spun earthward, and out of sight. And then another bomb dropped and another. Great, brown cylinders, noiselessly falling. The sun was blocked out by the mass.

Prickly shivers of fear, like little pins, poked at him, leaving him in a paralyzing stupor. He gawked at the *Luftwaffe* circling around, having lifted off for a counter attack.

Yes, the *Luftwaffe*! But, so few planes. Where was the rest of the fleet? The *Luftwaffe* was clearly outnumbered. "Quick," shouted SS Officer Spiegl, pointing to an underground tunnel entrance that led to a shelter.

Emil's body responded to the urgency in Spiegl's voice. There was no time for them to return to their stations, and only briefly did Emil wonder if they would be arrested for defeatism or cowardly acts, by not returning and retreating into a bomb shelter instead.

Nuremberg was famous for its system of underground cellars, built originally for the storage of beer, but now used to shelter citizens from bomb attacks. Several sections had be fortified as shelters. Civilians raced to the tunnels including the marked shelter Emil and his group entered.

"There's eleven feet of brick and concrete above us," one man said, comforting his frightened wife. "We will be okay."

"As long as it's not a direct hit," another man said, not so sensitive. "Otherwise, we might be trapped and suffocate."

"Please!" the first man said.

"I'm only stating the truth. Ostriches are not better off by sticking their heads in the sand."

The argument was cut short by a loud whistle, the loudest yet. Emil covered his ears to ease the pain. Then the earth shook. Large chunks of debris fell from the ceiling.

The women screamed, babies cried. The one light that lit the bunker died, throwing them all into total blackness. More screaming. Everyone ducked for cover, arms over heads, waiting for the explosions to cease.

And then it was over. Stillness. Quiet sobbing. SS Officer Spiegl climbed out of the shelter and pushed the door open, letting in a welcomed surge of air. Dust swirled throughout the tunnels, and out in the street; everything was coated in it. Emil brushed his sleeves, but that just created more dust. He stumbled around in a daze.

All the buildings up and down the block were destroyed; walls peeled away exposing the private lives of ordinary people. Beds, tables, cupboards ripped open.

Muffled cries grew into unbridled wailing.

"Help!" someone cried. "Over here!"

Not everyone had been lucky enough to make it to a shelter.

The youth from the Flak unit started hauling bricks away from a collapsed building. Someone was alive inside. Like worker bees, the people snapped to life, looking for survivors.

A shoe.

"I found someone!" Emil shouted. He dug madly to remove the bricks and mortar around the foot sticking out. Then he exposed the head and jumped back. A young boy, like Helmut, was crushed under the weight of the wall. Emil's eyes locked onto the boy's grey and bloodied face. His chest tightened and his stomach churned, pushing bile up this throat. The boy was dead. Crushed and bloody and dead.

"Come on, soldier," SS Officer Spiegl said. "They're moving the bodies over there."

He pointed to a row. A row of people. Dead.

Spiegl wanted Emil to touch it. He couldn't do it.

"Quickly!" he shouted. "Obey now!"

Emil forced himself, his hands shaking, to grab one of the boy's feet, then the other. He dragged him like a bag of flour, depositing the boy's crushed body in the row.

Tears threatened, and he bit his lip, forcing himself to focus. Crying was the ultimate weakness, and would not be tolerated.

He turned away from the bodies to search some more. It got easier after a while. More survivors, more casualties. More rows of corpses. They said it wasn't a bad hit. Berlin and Cologne had been worse.

But it was bad enough for him.

Chapter Thirty-One

For days afterward, instead of learning to fly, they cleaned up debris in the city. They did Flak training in the mornings, but what Emil really wanted was to be in a plane. He wanted *off* the ground, away from the nightmare below. He'd have to wait a little longer.

Georg turned out to be a walking encyclopedia. He loved to talk and he found great enjoyment in flaunting the fact that he knew more about a lot of things than Emil did.

"We won't go back to school. From here, it'll be the army."

"We're too young."

"We get older every day. Before you know it we'll be on the front, killing Soviets."

"You think we can win?"

"Of course. The *Fuehrer* has secret miracle weapons."

"Secret miracle weapons?"

"Yes, the *Fuehrer* is just waiting for the right time to use them."

Georg liked the sound of his own voice, Emil thought. He was always going off just when Emil was falling asleep. Sometimes, he wanted to climb to the top bunk and punch Georg in the stomach.

"You got a girl, Emil?"

"I'm trying to sleep."

"Is that a yes or no?"

Fake loud snore.

Georg laughed. "That must mean no. I got a girl. Nice sweet thing in Regensberg. I mean to marry her one day. Her name is Elisabeth Kramer."

"Kramer? Isn't that Jewish?"

"It's not always Jewish, you imbecile!"

With that, a pillow missile, hard across Emil's face.

"What? What's the matter with you, Georg?"

"You think I'd go with a Jewish dog? Besides, there's no Jews left in Germany. They're all dead. Dead in those concentration camps."

"What are you talking about?" Emil was awake now. "The Jews were resettled in Poland."

Georg laughed from the gut. Loud.

"Shut up, Georg."

"You are so gullible, Emil. I've never met anyone like you. The Jews are not resettling in Poland. That's the funniest thing I've ever heard. As if Hitler would give them anything. No, this is what they do to the Jews."

Georg dropped his head over the side. His face was upside down from Emil's perspective, his eyes wide and shaped like small rounded pockets. He reminded Emil of a demon. Like fireside ghost stories they used to tell as children, only then it was a pretend fear.

"They work them until they drop. Until they're bone skinny. Then they gas them and burn them in a furnace."

The image repulsed Emil. Georg was a storyteller, a liar, and he hated him for saying something so awful. "I don't believe you."

"It's true."

"How do you know? Who told you?"

His head disappeared. "Give me back my pillow."

171

Emil flicked it up. "How do you know about this, Georg?"

"I know people. Be quiet, Emil. I'm trying to sleep."

Now Emil really wanted to punch him in the stomach.

He thought of Anne and her family, of all the Jews who boarded the trains in Passau, so long ago, it felt like a whole other lifetime. Emil was afraid to fall asleep. He was afraid of what he might dream.

Except for the weekends at glider camp, Emil had never been away from home. Homesickness was a strange thing, he thought. You're not actually sick. You can't go to the nurse to get medicine for it. But it hurts. It hurts your stomach, it hurts your heart. And it's heavy, like a sack of flour on your back. It doesn't go away.

Small relief came in the form of letters from home. It proved to be just a teaser though, because the moment Emil finished reading, all the ache and heaviness came back, worse than before.

Bitter sweet. Like the first letter he'd gotten from Katharina.

May 16, 1943
Dear Emil,

How are you? Is life exciting for you in Nuremberg? I am doing as well as can be expected under the circumstances. I get up before dawn to work on the farm, and work until dusk. Not a lot of time for fun. I haven't gone to the theater since you left. Once a week my mother and I go to the spoiled food depot hoping to get a bag of sugar or block of margarine with our food rationing coupons. Those things are really worthless, but I will refrain from saying more. We get up very early to stand in line because if we're lucky enough to get something, it's better than a bucket of money. We can trade with a bag of sugar for weeks.

Johann is at an army base in Regensberg. We don't hear from him enough, and I worry about him. I worry about you, too. I wish you were here.

Please be safe.

Love Katharina.

Love Katharina? *Love?* Well, there are all kinds of love, Emil reasoned. She probably just loved him like a brother, a friend. *Could it be more?* She was worried about him. She wished he were there.

He was being stupid. She was worried about Johann, too. He was nothing special. *Was he?* He was very confused. How should he write her back?

Emil sat down at the desk and removed a clean sheet of paper from the drawer. With pen in hand, he began:

June 11, 1943

Dear Katharina,

It is so good to get a letter from you. I miss everyone so much. We work hard here, too. Up early for breakfast and exercise and then to train with the Flak guns. In the afternoons, we study flight training. Haven't flown yet. It's surprising how few planes are actually stationed here.

Emil knew his letter could be censored and considered scratching the last line out. But, he left it in. Let them scratch it out if they don't like it.

Mostly, it's the agony of just waiting for something to happen. We were bombed the first day...

Should he write details? He didn't want to scare her. Probably not. For sure the censors didn't want him to spread word about the fear and carnage of that day.

...but I'm fine.

Just leave it at that. He didn't want to lie to her either.

Chances are we won't get hit again, but that's why I'm here. To man the Flak. Just in case. So every day I get up wondering, will it just be training today, or the real thing?

I wish I were there to go to the theater with you, or just be together.

Was that too obvious? Too sentimental? Should he tell her how he really felt? What if he died in the next bombing without telling her that he liked her more than a friend?

Next letter, he decided. He would wait for her reply; maybe she would give him more clues as to her true feelings for him.

My best regards,
Emil

My best regards? My best *regards?* After she said *love?* What if she interprets that as his not being interested in her? *Only friends?*

He decided to squeeze in a small *"with love"* above his name. He hoped it didn't look silly.

Chapter Thirty-Two

"Emil!"

Emil spun on his heel, shocked to see the man who walked up from behind him.

"Onkel Rudi?" A smile spread across Emil's face. "*Hallo*."

Onkel Rudi grabbed his hand with a confident shake. "*Mein Gott*, Emil, you have grown into a man!"

"Yes, thank you."

Onkel Rudi, on the other hand seemed to have shriveled. Emil remembered him from his visit to their house long ago, so strong, assured, and virile. Now he looked as if someone had punched him in the stomach. He slouched, his shoulders slumped forward, the skin on his face hung loose.

"So, you are here to man the Flak guns?" Onkel Rudi asked.

What was that expression on his face? Emil thought. *Concern?*

"I am. And to train as a pilot for the *Luftwaffe*," Emil added proudly.

"Yes, I see," Onkel Rudi said. "For the *Fuehrer*."

"For the *Fuehrer*."

Gone was the enthusiasm Onkel Rudi had exhibited back in Passau, when he told tales of amazing adventure and danger while bombing Poland. He just stared at Emil for a few seconds; Emil scrambled for something to say. "Are you here long?"

"Just a day."

"Oh." Then an idea. "Can you take me for a ride in your plane?"

Onkel Rudi laughed. "It's too dangerous, Emil. If the enemy didn't shoot us down, our own Flaks would. For wasting the Reich's fuel."

He was right. Emil offered a rueful smile back.

"It was good to see you again," he said.

Emil shifted his weight then looked the older man in the eyes. "You, too."

Onkel Rudi clicked his heels and saluted, "*Heil Hitler!*"

Obediently Emil returned the gesture and watched him leave.

The alarm went off in the middle of the night.

"This is not a drill!" Someone shouted in the hall. "This is not a drill!"

Emil and Georg scrambled to their feet, changing clumsily into their uniforms, rushing with their boots straps, and grabbing their metal helmets on the way out. They knew exactly where to go and made their way to Station Three. SS Officer Spiegl, who was positioned as the gun commander, was already there with a third youth. He had his headphones on receiving information as to location. Emil and Georg worked with the third guy, to load the rounds.

Emil's head spun. *Was this happening? Was he really going to shoot a British fighter plane out of the sky?*

No time to think. The searchlight crews scattered around the city snapped on their lights. They were spaced five kilometers apart in a chessboard pattern across Nuremberg. Together they "coned" their beams to illuminate enemy bombers.

"FIRE!"

They lit the fuse and the canon fired. Emil pressed his hands against his ears and ducked down.

Secretly he hoped they missed. He couldn't forget that Moritz had died because they didn't believe in this war.

"Again!" SS Officer Spiegl shouted.

They loaded the next round. The bombs hit hard around them. The ground shook and the sky turned orange. Shrapnel whizzed by. Emil squatted down low.

"FIRE!"

They lit the fuse.

Miss, Emil thought. Miss. Miss.

At the same time he hated what the Allies were doing to Nuremberg. Bomb after bomb. Explosion, loud hissing, bright heat. *Stop. Please stop.*

"Again!"

Another load. Another fuse lit.

"We got it!" Georg cheered. They all ducked down and watched the Royal Air Force plane plunge to the ground. More cheering.

"Again!"

It seemed it wouldn't stop. Emil's heart raced, his hands shook. He couldn't get the image of that plane exploding and falling out of his mind. All he could think about was how disappointed Johann would be if he knew.

Chapter Thirty-Three

J*uly 2, 1943*

Dear Mother,

You've probably heard about the recent bombing in Nuremberg. I wanted you to know that I am all right. Bombing does a terrible thing to a city. I understand now why you cried when we invaded Poland.

Don't worry that you haven't heard from Father. With so many roads and railways out, it's hard for the post to get through, especially from the east.

Love Emil

"Firestorm, Emil, a *firestorm*. The allies dropped incendiary bombs on Hamburg, thousands of them."

Emil could count on Georg to update him. "What's an incendiary bomb?"

Georg looked at Emil like he was an infant.

"They're chemicals. Chemicals that blow up when they hit the ground and spread lots of hot, hot fire."

Georg was too agitated to climb up to his bunk, or to sit at the desk.

"Forty thousand people died. A bloody inferno."

"What about the bomb shelters. Didn't that save some?"

"No, that's the thing. The bomb shelters were useless. Everyone suffocated or burnt to death. The heat was so hot, people melted. *Melted*, Emil."

"Are you sure?" *How did Georg know these things?*

"Yes, I'm sure. It's on the radio, in the newspaper."

It must really be bad if it made the German news, Emil thought. Propaganda usually reports on victories, unless the truth is too big to hide.

"Corpses are shriveled to half their normal size; clothes burned right off their bodies. Forty thousand people."

"Georg." Stop, please. This was terrible. Emil's stomach churned, he was dizzy and dropped onto his bed. Georg's graphic images made him sick.

It was hard not to hate the Allies now.

The summer of 1943 saw the defeat of the German Central Army on the eastern front. The Germans called it Operation Citadel and it was meant to demonstrate Germany's strength and determination to achieve ultimate victory. It was the largest tank war to date and it turned out that the Red Army was a tank-making machine. Reports were that the Soviets produced two thousand tankers a month. Germany only produced half as many. Over nine hundred Soviet tankers exploded onto the warpath in that battle.

After losing Stalingrad, this loss was particularly painful to the German campaign in the east. To make matters much worse, the Allies occupied Sicily around the same time. Germany had to fight on two fronts; men were sent from the eastern front to support the south, men the central army could ill afford to give up.

179

By autumn it became apparent to all but fanatics like Georg, that Germany was losing the war. After the allies landed in Italy, they systematically pushed their offensive line further north, approaching from both the south and west. On October 13, Italy declared war on Germany. The *Fuehrer*'s strongest alliance had turned against him.

"Mussolini was dead weight," Georg declared when he heard the news. "Germany is stronger without him."

It was funny how Georg could be so smart, Emil thought, and yet so stupid.

Emil was surprised when they offered him a three-day leave for Christmas. A ball of homesickness hung in his gut, and with the first sight of Passau—the beautiful brassy blue towers of St. Stephens Dome frosted with snow, the merging of the Danube and the Inn Rivers—his body trembled. He wanted to jump out of the train and kiss the ground. He felt like he could breathe again.

His family was at the train station to greet him.

"Mother! Helmut!"

"Emil!" They yelled. Helmut jumped him, almost knocking him to the ground. He must have grown thirty centimeters since Emil last saw him.

"Helmut, you're so tall."

"Hey, I'm almost as tall as you!"

"Almost," Emil said grinning.

Mother tenderly wrapped her arms around Emil, and wept softly. "You are an answer to prayer, son. I was praying that you could come home for Christmas."

180

She took a step back. "You look good. I'm glad to see they are taking care of you in Nuremberg."

Emil wished he could say the same about her. She was even thinner than before, if that were possible, but her shoulders were straight and her expression strong. She was not the type of person to go down without a fight.

"And more good news!" she said, waving an opened envelope. "I finally got a letter from your father. He is still alive. Having you home, Emil and knowing your father is alive, is all I wanted for Christmas this year!"

Her eyes actually sparkled. Even in the darkness of this terrible war, Mother could find joy.

Emil glanced around the train station, half-hoping that maybe Katharina had come too, but glad she hadn't. He didn't want their reunion to play out in front of his mother and little brother.

Emil did make an excuse to go see her, though. Johann was home, too, so Mother and Helmut were none the wiser about his desire to see her.

Even though it was winter, Emil rode his bike through the slush and snow, but he stopped when he spotted their farm.

He told himself to breathe. He also wanted to see Johann, and it wasn't like he was nervous to see him. He just had to focus on Johann. His old buddy Johann.

Pushing his bike down the drive to their house Emil saw him. He knew it was Johann because he was wearing his brown army uniform. His back was turned to Emil and he was carrying a pitchfork.

"Hey, Johann!"

Johann spun around. "Emil, my friend!"

Emil shook Johann's hand vigorously.

I missed you," Johann said. "I mean, I was kind of sick of you when you left…"

Emil punched him playfully in the arm. "What'd you mean? I was the one that had to stare at the back of your head every day."

"What? This handsome head. It was a privilege for you."

Laughing, Emil followed him to the barn. "So, how's the army been treating you?"

"Ah, you know." He lowered his voice, "It's not like I'm actually going to fight."

What did he mean by that? Did he think the war would be over, or was he just going to refuse when the time came? A final resistance of sorts. They were sixteen now. Anything could happen.

Emil didn't want to dim the mood with a serious conversation so he didn't question Johann further. They were both only home for a short time. Emil was saved by the sudden appearance of Katharina.

With the sun shimmering from behind, she looked angelic. He gasped at her beauty and it took a moment before he could find his voice.

"Hello," he finally mustered.

"Emil!" To his utter amazement and absolute joy, she rushed to embrace him. Christmas couldn't get any better than this.

"It's so good to see you," she said. "I heard you had leave."

"It's really great to see you, too," Emil said, all but forgetting that Johann was standing there.

"Well, aren't you two a sight," Johann said, grinning slyly. "If you don't mind, and I'm sure you don't, I'll just make myself busy, over here, in the barn. Just in case you're wondering." He laughed and sauntered off.

The affection Emil had for Katharina was pretty obvious. He couldn't hide how seeing her made him feel, and he was overjoyed to see she was struggling with the same thing.

They started walking, slowly, down the drive, and she asked him about Nuremberg, he about her family and plans for Christmas.

"Pretty simple, like most folks, I imagine," she said. "A small meal, worship. We're just happy to be together."

Emil nodded. "Us, too. Except, you know, Father is still away."

"I'm sorry he couldn't get leave. Is he well?"

"Yes, at least I think so. Mother received a letter from him recently, but it was written some time ago."

Out of the corner of his eye Emil saw movement, two men he didn't recognize working in the fields.

"Who's that?"

"That? Two Frenchies, POWs sent to help with the farm. They're everywhere now, alien prisoners from France, Belgium, and Holland. Even some from the east.

They are sent here to work because of the shortage of manpower."

"Is it safe? I mean for you?"

She laughed. "I'm never alone with either of them. My mother sees to that. But it is disgusting how some of the girls flirt with the foreigners."

Alarming news.

"Oh, no. I'm not like that. Besides it's against the law. Fraternizing with the enemy is a criminal offense. I've heard that some unscrupulous farm wives have been arrested."

"Where do the prisoners stay?"

"In the loft."

"Our loft?" It was unreasonable, Emil knew, but he felt violated.

"I know. I'm sad we can't go there anymore, too."

"I want you to keep your distance from them, okay?"

She smiled and grabbed his arm. "You're worried about me. That's so sweet."

"Just promise me."

"I promise."

Katharina wore a thin winter jacket over her mid-length dress. It was chilly enough to see their breath and she was shivering. "You're cold," Emil said. "We should go back."

"I'm okay."

"No, you're shivering. At least let me give you my coat."

"Then you'd be cold, and you'd have to go. How about we just walk a little closer together?"

Emil put his arm around her shoulder. "Like this? Is this okay?"

"That's fine," she said. "Thank you. I'm much warmer now."

The funny thing was, so was he.

Like other soldiers on leave, Emil was able to bring home a small package of food, items no longer available to common civilians.

He had a tin of canned meat and a small jar of peaches. Mother had managed to find a loaf of bread and another pat of butter.

She set the table carefully, but Emil noted all of their good silverware was missing. He also wondered why she put out five settings.

"I invited Frau Schwarz and Karl."

Emil felt annoyed. They hardly had enough food for the three of them, and he wanted mother and Helmut all to himself.

"Don't they have their own family?"

Mother paused to consider him. "No. I don't think you heard about Herr Schwarz. They sent word three weeks ago. He died in France."

"Oh." *Herr Schwarz was dead?* Emil liked the man and was saddened by the news. He felt bad for Frau Schwarz and Karl and was glad now, that they were joining his family for dinner.

"What about Tante Gerta?" Helmut asked.

"She doesn't believe in Christmas," said Mother. "She took an extra shift at the prison." She scowled as she thought about it. "I don't even want to know what she does there."

The Schwarz family arrived. Helmut was happy to see Karl, and he showed him a strangely shaped rock he had found on the farm where he worked.

"Thank you so much for inviting us over, Leni." Frau Schwarz eyes were pools of sadness. "It was very kind of you."

They sat around the table and Emil lit the candles. Mother presented the food in small slices and portions over three plates so that it actually looked like there was more food than there really was.

And as usual, she prayed.

The food was delicious. The bread and butter, the sliced canned ham, the sweetness of the peaches. The smiles all around made it a perfect Christmas Eve dinner. And to Emil's surprise, there was enough for everyone.

It was Christmas, 1943. That meant a church service at 18:00 at St. Matthew's Lutheran Church.

Emil and Helmut stomped the snow off their boots and followed Mother inside. They were accustomed to sitting on the left-hand side, mid way up, and that was where Mother led them again. Emil was surprised at how full it was. He assumed the war had more people praying.

Pastor Kuhnhauser sat in the front row. He was an old man with thick jowls, a fixture in Emil's life, and the only pastor St. Matthew's Lutheran Church had had since he'd been born. The kind of person you thought would never die. He had a Bible in his lap, his bald head bowed over it, praying.

He stood up, and on cue Frau Koning rose to play the organ.

Christmas Carols. *What a comfort to sing the songs of my childhood again*, Emil thought. *Stille Nacht, Heilige Nacht*. Silent Night, Holy Night, All is calm. All is bright…

Pastor Kuhnhauser walked to the pulpit.

"Greetings in the name of Jesus Christ, whose birthday we are celebrating."

Emil held his breath. Little red flags. No *Heil Hitler*? Will he at least bless the Third Reich?

"God so loved the world, that he gave his one and only son, that whoever believes in him shall not perish but have eternal life. He came in the form of an infant…"

Emil exhaled. Okay, a normal Christmas tale.

"Though God's son, he was rejected by the rulers of the day."

Emil shifted uncomfortably.

"He came for sinners, to save them from the consequences of their sins, and if ever we needed someone to save us from our sins, it is today."

The pastor continued. "I must confess. I have waited far too long to speak. I have let the fear of man and not the fear of God rule my heart."

Emil's heart pounded in his chest. *Oh, no, oh no, oh no.*
"A terrible evil has overcome us."

A shuffle in the back of the room. Emil swiveled his neck. Two SS Officers wearing their usual black coats stood in the back. *Stop Pastor, stop!*

"We must not remain silent while a plot to ruin a whole people is being carried out, right under our noses."

Emil heard someone behind him whisper, "What is he talking about?" But Emil knew. *Damn Georg Stramm was right again.*

"Especially to attack God's chosen race, the Jewish people, like Jesus, himself."

The Black Coats in the back began to speak together, but Emil couldn't hear what they said.

"Confess your sins to one another." Pastor Kuhnhauser 's voice was surprisingly calm. "And he will forgive you. He is faithful and kind. He longs to gather you under his wings like a hen gathers together her chicks."

He fixed his gaze on the Black Coats with an intensity that made Emil's skin chill. "But he is also holy and just. And he will bring justice to this earth."

"Halt!" A Black Coat called out in response. "You must stop speaking!"

"Faithful flock, do not forsake the gathering of yourselves together. Keep the faith. Do the good work."

The Black Coats stormed towards the altar. Emil looked at Mother. Her eyes were tearing up, but her expression wasn't fear. *Was it pride?*

"Love one another as God has loved you!"

Those were his last words.

The Black Coats strapped his arms behind his back but Pastor Kuhnhauser remained calm. He exited the building with his head high and his eyes shining.

He had accomplished what he had set out to do.

Word of Pastor Kuhnhauser's arrest spread through town. Emil feared there would be some kind of spiritual which would mean more arrests and executions, for there was not a doubt in his mind that the Nazis had just made their pastor a martyr.

Chapter Thirty-Four

1944
FEBRUARY

The early morning silence normally found at the Nuremberg base was broken by a fit of coughing. It came from deep in Emil's chest, wet and violent, thrusting him into a sitting position out of a fitful sleep. Each cough pierced his lungs painfully, and a loud groan escaped after a particularly brutal bout.

"Shut up, Emil!" Georg showed no mercy. The joints of the overhead bunk squeaked as the weight of his body rolled over.

Emil concentrated carefully, willing his chest to calm. Moist lines streamed down his cheeks and for one mortifying moment, Emil thought he'd started crying.

But it was sweat running off his forehead into his eyes. He threw his sheet off with a flick of his leg, lying exposed in his underwear. *Who'd turned on the heat?*

By morning, Georg was coughing, too, and by the end of the day, half the barrack lay sick in their bunks. Pneumonia had spread across the camp.

The bad news was the Nazi regime didn't want to pay for them to regain their health. The burden would belong to their families. The good news: Emil was going back to Passau.

He barely remembered the train ride home, only how soothing the cool glass of the window felt against his cheek. He didn't remember being picked up by Mother and Helmut, or how he'd made it to his bed.

Vaguely he'd been aware of someone holding his head up to sip water—his tongue running along the rough chapped surface of his lips—and tapping his brow with a cool cloth. But mostly he slept, oblivious to the fact that the war had indeed found its way to their corner of Germany. That Johann and Katharina's father had been killed when a bomb landed on the orchestra playing in Munich, that food trucks no longer cared about the people of Passau, and that Allied bombers were flying ever closer.

One day the shadow in his room spoke to him. "Emil? Can you hear me?"

Emil felt his eye lids flutter as he struggled to open them. He knew this voice. "Mother?"

"Yes, Emil, I'm here. Oh, son. You're going to be okay."

Emil sensed something in her voice. *Happiness? Relief?*

Eventually the weight on his lungs lifted. He could draw breath in deeply, and the heat in his body subsided.

One day when Helmut brought him a bowl of thin soup, Emil inquired about the Ackermanns.

"Johann is home on leave," Helmut said, settling into a wooden kitchen chair their mother had carried up. "Mother told him we'd let them know when you were well enough for a visit."

"I'm well enough," Emil said, desperate to see Katharina again. And Johann too, of course. "Go tell them."

Johann and Katharina arrived later that afternoon. In his mind, Katharina would walk through his bedroom door, pausing briefly before flinging her body over his, weeping for joy that he still lived.

In reality she hesitated, letting Johann take the lead. She didn't fling herself, or even touch him. Her eyes reflected melancholy when she smiled.

"Hey, old man," Johann joked. "Nice of you to make room in your busy schedule for us."

"Yeah, well, you can see I've been busy. Thanks for coming."

Emil shifted his gaze from Johann's to Katharina's.

"Hello, Emil."

"Hello."

"I'm so happy to hear that you are feeling better."

"It's good to be home."

Emil was surprised by the awkwardness in the room, like they hadn't grown up together. Like they hadn't been best friends. Like they hadn't wrote those letters.

"Well," Johann said, "don't get well too quickly. They'll just send you back once they get wind of any sign of good health."

Emil grunted. "I'll do my best."

The room was grey even though Mother had opened the blinds, and Emil could feel the cold air that whistled through the window panes.

"Mother told me about your father," Emil said. "I'm sorry."

Johann and Katharina both stared at their feet. Katharina bit her lip, pinching her eyes shut.

"Thanks," Johann finally said. "It's the irony of war. Those who want to live, die. Those who want to die, live on."

"Oh, I don't know, Johann. Death is pretty indiscriminate, as far as I can tell."

Johann shoved his hands into his jacket pockets. "I wonder what Moritz would think if he were here now."

"It seems like just yesterday we were at his house listening to the BBC," Emil said. "Although, I remember us being a whole lot smaller."

"That's how I remember him," Katharina added softly. "A little boy. Never to be a man."

"He's lucky in a way," said Johann. "He didn't have to see what's become of Germany. It would've broken his heart."

"It breaks all our hearts," said Katharina.

"I can't believe we actually did what we did back then," added Johann.

"If we knew how bad it was going to get," Emil said, "we probably would have done more."

"We can't be too hard on ourselves," Katharina said. "We were only kids. We're still only kids."

Emil thought Johann would leave him and Katharina alone for a little while before they left, but to his disappointment, they said good-bye and left together.

Things had changed between him and Katharina, and if there was ever anything special growing between them, he felt sure it was gone now.

Chapter Thirty-Five

MARCH

It was a daily struggle to survive. Food was scarce to non-existent. The bombs fell all around them, sometimes too close for comfort. Because of his illness, Emil couldn't make it to the shelter down the street on time. He had to go down into their own cellar for protection.

Begging Mother and Helmut to leave him was futile so they would sit together in the damp, cool basement, where the vegetables were once kept from freezing during the winters.

The piercing cry of the sirens rang out again. The coldness of the room scratched at his lungs. They huddled together crouching down on the exposed earth and waited.

The earth trembled. Close, but not a direct hit. It was as if Passau was just target practice for bigger centers like Munich or Nuremberg.

Emil stared at the potato bin. Nothing but potatoes since he'd arrived from Nuremberg. Mother gave thanks *before* making the meal now. Emil could see why. There were only a few left. He could see the bottom of the bin. They would surely starve to death before the war was over.

As it was, after the sirens stopped, Helmut grabbed three potatoes for their mid-day meal. Now Emil was really worried.

Before they ate, Mother and Helmut bowed their heads to pray again. To be polite, Emil said Amen along with them.

"I hate to bring this up," Emil started. "But at this rate, we will be out of potatoes by the end of the week. Did you not notice that the bin is nearly empty?"

Helmut and Mother exchanged glances.

"God is our provider, Emil," Mother said. Now, Emil wanted to respect her faith but in this case he was certain she was misguided. If they didn't find more food soon, they were in trouble. Helmut interrupted his thoughts.

"The bin's been like that for weeks."

"Been like what?"

"Nearly empty."

"How could that be possible?"

Helmut shrugged. "I don't know. It just never goes empty."

Could that be true? Emil looked at Mother. She didn't contradict him. And if there was one thing Emil knew about Mother, she didn't lie.

A short while after the sirens ended, Katharina knocked on the door.

"The planes are gone, and it's spring," she started. "I wondered if you'd like to go for a walk. That is if you feel up to it."

"Yes," Emil answered quickly. "I feel fine."

He grabbed a jacket and joined Katharina as they walked down the cobbled street. The breezed still blew cool, but the sun on his face felt hopeful. They walked slowly. Even though Emil wanted to proclaim good health, his lungs still protested and his body lacked its former strength.

"I'm sorry I've been avoiding you," Katharina said.

"I've noticed that. Why?"

"People are dying. I just thought that maybe it would be better not to get too close."

Emil stopped. "You miss your father."

She let her gaze fall. "Yes, I do. Very much. I think of him every day."

Then she looked him in the eyes. "I'm afraid of losing the people I love."

The people I love, he thought. *Me?*

Emil took a chance and reached for her hand. "I understand. There are no guarantees. But, you really have no choice."

"What do you mean?"

"We've been through too much already. Been friends too long. The damage has already been done."

197

She smiled. "I see."

They walked hand in hand to the end of the street, Katharina matching his gait, comfortably silent.

At the end Emil turned to her.

His second biggest fear after death was dying without ever having kissed a girl. Without ever having kissed Katharina.

She tilted her head up to his and Emil knew this was it. He leaned in to kiss her. Her lips were soft and sweet and he melted, his whole body tingling with warmth.

She pulled away and smiled shyly. "I should go back."

They walked back to Emil's front door grinning, feeling happy like the war wasn't going on at all.

"Will I see you tomorrow?" he asked. *And every day after that, please?*

"Yes. I'll see you again tomorrow." She waved as she turned the corner out of sight.

Emil saw Katharina often after that. She either stopped in so Emil could join her on an errand into town, or Emil rode his bike to the farm to see her, his lungs growing stronger each day. They were at war, and there wasn't much time for leisure, so they spent most of their time working together, usually on the farm. Emil didn't mind the work so much as long as they were together. Still recovering from his illness, he was relegated to the barn, pitching hay or gathering eggs. The Reich had supplied the Ackermanns with more hens and an extra milking cow, but

198

most of the goods were still shipped out of town. There was a thriving black market going on as well. Eggs and milk slipped away out of the view of the officers who milled around. Most of them were locals, and turned a blind eye, knowing that an extra egg or two could end up on their table.

At the end of each day, Emil would kiss Katharina good night.

"Do you think they'll let you stay?" she whispered one night. He knew she meant the army. His cough had subsided and the doctor had declared him well. Johann had returned weeks ago and the army was desperate for soldiers. It was just a matter of time.

"I'm not fit for the front, but I'm still useful to them, I think," he said.

"I hope you don't go." She embraced him, holding tight. Emil held her back and kissed the top of her head. All he wanted was to take her away to some safe place and just love her. His body tensed with anger that he was helpless to do this.

"I'm not gone, yet." Emil lifted her chin and forced a smile. "Let's not worry about tomorrow, okay?"

Chapter Thirty-Six

MAY

S trafing aircraft could come at anytime. Small, low-flying planes, sometimes American, sometimes British, would buzz over towns, over fields, indiscriminately firing their machine guns.

Emil thought they were worse than the bombers in that there was seldom a siren for warnings. They were safe, and then suddenly they weren't.

Perhaps the Allies did this to break the psyche of the German people, Emil mused. Perhaps they just got bored in between bombings, and target shooting the enemy provided them with a bit of fun.

Sometimes, if they were lucky, Passau residents heard them coming in time to hide in a barn or bombed-out cellar.

Helmut and Karl went scavenging for food every afternoon before their evening shifts at the searchlight battery. Emil happened to be on his bicycle riding back from the Ackermann's when he spotted them, digging, looking for turnips or carrots, any type of root vegetable that may be thriving, hidden underground.

He stopped and waved.

"Hey, Helmut! Karl!"

They waved back. Watching his little brother, Emil was overcome with pride. He worked as hard as any soldier, truly taking the place of the man of the house while Emil and Father were gone. He looked after Mother, and did his duties to protect Germany. Emil felt sorrow, too. Helmut never had a chance to be a child. No time to be free of worry and fear and responsibility and by the time this war was over, his chance at childhood would be gone for good.

A low rumbling, a buzzing motorized hum.

Oh, no.

"Helmut! Helmut!" Emil pointed up. They saw it, too. They started to run, but were caught, out in the middle of the field.

"Run, run!" Emil shouted dropping his bike. He ran, but they were too far. His lungs burned. He fell to the ground as the plane closed in. It swooped lower and fired. Helmut and Karl dropped to the dirt, arms over head. Two rows of ammunition hit the field, *rat-tat-tat-tat, rat-tat-tat-tat,* spraying dust into the air.

Then it was gone. Emil picked himself up, his heart racing, fear prickling every inch of his body. The boys remained on the ground.

Get up. Get up!

Helmut lifted his head, flinging dirt out of his hair. Emil breathed out in relief. He sprinted to his side.

"Helmut! Are you okay?"

His little brother shifted more, pushing himself up. "Karl?"

Helmut and Emil reached Karl at the same time. He was face down. Red dots spotted his back.

"Karl!" Helmut turned him over. "Oh, no!" he cried. "Karl, no."

Karl's chest oozed with blood. It remained still, not rising with breath.

Emil laid a trembling hand on Helmut's shoulder. "I'm sorry."

"Why, Emil? Why?"

"I don't know."

Poor Helmut, Emil thought. Sometimes a man, sometimes a child, now a bit of both. *I don't know how to help you.*

"He was my best friend," Helmut cried. Tears poured down his face, drawing white streaks through the dust on his skin.

"I need him, Emil. I need him." Helmut bent over Karl's body and sobbed.

Emil had to help his mother hold Frau Schwarz up at Karl's short funeral, her legs buckling under her weight as she sobbed openly. For days afterward, Helmut seemed to curl up inside himself, his chin heavy against his chest as he dutifully completed the tasks the *Deutsches Jungvolk* required of him. Emil wished there was something he could do to bring cheer to his family, but the regime had other plans.

A notice came for him in the mail. The army had determined that Emil was well enough to get back into the fight. They were sending him back to Nuremberg.

"I can't believe you're leaving again," Katharina said softly. Emil took her hand and weaved his fingers through hers. He couldn't believe it either. Tomorrow he'd be gone.

They strolled through the park by St. Stephens along the riverside. From here, downtown Passau looked locked in time, unscathed by war. Emil wished he could keep this moment locked away, too.

"Everything just seems so hopeless," Katharina said.

The mood in the nation was the gloomiest it had ever been in more than four years of war. Everyone felt overwhelming despair. Emil could see it in the hollowness of their eyes, in the shuffle of their walk.

"It can't be much longer now, can it?" Katharina said. "A year maybe?"

The end of the war. It was the only thing on everyone's mind.

"I hope so. Maybe less." Emil wished he could comfort her in some way, but he had nothing to offer her. Nothing at all.

"I wonder what it will be like," she said. "I guess it means every German, you, me, everyone, will be prisoners of war."

"Let's just pray it's the Americans or the British that capture us."

"Why?"

Emil shrugged. "I've heard things." *The brutality of the Reds.* "I don't know. Either way, it won't be good."

"It's so depressing." She stopped and looked at him then. "You know, I like to dream about a different world. One where I get married, have children, build a home in a place where bombs aren't falling. Where I'm not afraid all the time. Is that crazy? Am I a child?"

"I love you." Emil blurted out. "I want to marry you." He couldn't stop himself. He'd thought about it all the time, about her. He shared her dream of a life after the war. He didn't know if he'd still be here then, but he wanted to be, really wanted to be, because of her.

She burst out crying.

"Katharina?" *Was he wrong?*

"Oh, Emil. I love you, too."

She kissed him hard and his nerves exploded. He wanted to take her away right then and there, but Katharina was not a wanton girl like Irmgard. That was what Emil loved about her.

"I wish I could give you something to remember this day by, so that you won't forget me," he said.

"We could do as the Americans do," Katharina said with a twinkle in her eye. She tugged a loose blue string that hung button-free on her coat. She held it in the air, smiling.

Understanding, Emil took it and carefully and wrapped it around her finger.

"Voila," Emil said.

"It's perfect," Katharina gushed.

He tied a knot, making sure the string wasn't wrapped too tightly, but secure enough that it wouldn't fall off. "You are spoken for, young lady."

Katharina held her hand out in front as if she were showing off a ten karat diamond. "That I am."

Later that night Emil told his mother he'd asked Katharina to marry him. A part of him was afraid she would chastise him for being silly—that sixteen was too young.

But nobody was young anymore.

Mother just hugged him and told him congratulations. Saying good-bye to him again was more than enough for her to deal with in that moment.

At the train station the next day, she and Helmut said good-bye with big hugs and tears and wished Emil well, leaving before the train arrived so he could have the last few precious minutes with Katharina.

Her cheeks were damp with tears, and he kissed the salty wetness away, holding her tight.

"It will be okay," he soothed. "We will see each other again soon. Remember, only a year and then our life together can begin."

"Only a year."

It might be a dream, but they were dreaming it together.

The train arrived and Emil boarded. As he watched Katharina disappear into the distance, his heart stretched and tore like a rubber band and he thought he might vomit in the chair beside him.

Chapter Thirty-Seven

AUGUST

Officer Spiegl looked strange. His broad shoulders slumped inward slightly and his brow crease was more severe. For the first time Emil sensed a certain weariness in him.

"Men," he began. With this small word, Emil knew there was trouble. Officer Spiegl always called them boys or at best, young men, but never simply men.

"It is my duty to inform you that you will soon have the privilege of fighting in our great *Fuehrer*'s army. The battle in the east continues to rage, and you will go to serve the Fatherland there, as you should. Germany owes you nothing. The Fatherland has given you everything and in turn it requires everything from you."

A murmur rippled through the ranks. Everyone had heard the fight on the eastern front in the Ukraine was not going well. And that most men who went there, never returned.

"Pack your things," Officer Spiegl instructed. "And prepare to be transferred to Nuremberg's army training camp."

Chairs scraped across the wooden floor, boots shuffled as their owners shifted in agitation or excitement, maybe both.

"We can yet win this war!" Spiegl bellowed. "We must yet win this war! We will show the world the strength of spirit left in Germany!"

Applause broke out timidly, first one then two, until the whole room had joined in, clapping. They cheered, "Germany, Germany, above all others!"

They were flight students; they manned the Flak guns. Now they would be foot soldiers.

If there was anything good about this news, Emil thought, it was that they were to be joined by a group of army youth from Passau. Emil would see Johann again. The bad news was he would be seeing Friedrich again, too.

Emil went with Spiegl to meet them at the train station. They waited in the wing that hadn't been blown out in the last raid. Men worked to clean up the rubble, but the once efficient running and pristine station reminded Emil of the many wounded soldiers that hobbled about, forced to function as before but without a limb.

Being alone with Officer Spiegl was awkward. He stood still, shoulders back, legs apart, statue-like. Emil copied his demeanor, thankful that nothing inspired the officer to chat. Officer Spiegl requested that Emil join him because he was from Passau and could accurately identify the "men" who would be arriving from there.

Emil kept looking at the station's clock, willing the train from Passau to arrive on time. The once well-oiled-runs-like-clockwork transportation network could no longer be counted on. He heard the whistle before he recognized the mop of hair sticking out of one of the windows.

"Emil!" Johann jumped off the ramp and gave Emil a strong handshake. "It's so great to see you again!"

If it weren't for Officer Spiegl standing right there, Emil would've given Johann a bear hug. Maybe even a kiss on the cheek. Though it'd only been four months since they'd seen each other, it felt like years.

Instead he heartily pumped his friend's arm. "You're looking, good, Johann."

They were accompanied by several other boys from their army unit, all greeting Emil and Officer Spiegl stoically.

"Hello, Emil." It was Friedrich. He punched Emil playfully in the shoulder like they were old friends. A little too hard, it stung, but Emil wouldn't give Friedrich the pleasure of knowing so by rubbing it.

"Friedrich, I didn't believe it was possible, but you've grown." He was still skinny as a whip, Emil thought, but taller, his legs and arms lanky appendages. Strong though, Emil reminded himself, as his arm pulsed from their greeting.

Emil and Georg had built another set of bunk beds in their room to accommodate Friedrich and Johann. The room was barely large enough for the first set; now they could hardly walk between them, and certainly not two at a time.

Georg and Friedrich claimed the top bunks, lying back with their hands behind their heads, as if they hadn't a worry in the world. It took all of ten minutes for them to start talking propaganda and arms. Emil should have known those two would hit it off.

209

"Emil," Johann said, "Where are the toilets?" Emil gave him directions, down the hall to the left.

"He's such a pansy," Friedrich said when Johann left the room.

"What?"

"Johann."

Friedrich didn't know about their clandestine meetings, Emil thought, or the flyers Johann had delivered illegally. That took guts. Friedrich was an idiot.

"He's no such thing!" Emil snapped back.

Friedrich wouldn't relent. "Johann's a weakling. A weak link."

A slippery smile crossed Georg's face. He loved confrontation.

Emil stood as tall as he could and thrust his chin out. "You mess with him, you mess with me."

"Whoa, slow down," Friedrich said, chuckling. "We're on the same team. We're from the same town, practically brothers."

Brothers? Emil thought. *Over my dead body.*

Rifle and machine gun practice, sprints and pushups, map reading of the eastern targets, basic Russian, panzer tank mechanic instruction, grenades; for the next three weeks they trained from dusk to dawn, pushing their minds and bodies with little sleep in between. It made their Hitler Youth exercises seem like kindergarten.

The last night before they left to fight, Spiegl took them to the local bar so they could drink beer and smoke cigarettes.

"You were right, Johann," Emil said, resting against the bar, so tired he could barely keep his head from dropping onto the tabletop.

"About?"

"Here we are, off to battle. I thought we were too young, that we'd be spared. But you were right. You knew they were going to make us fight."

"I didn't know," Johann said. "I just hoped I'd be wrong. Maybe saying it aloud cursed us. I should've just kept my mouth shut."

"So, you're trying to take responsibility for *this*, now?" Emil said, a small grin forming. "I hate to be the one to break it to you..."

"I know *I* didn't cause this to happen. You know what I mean. I'm just tired." Johann laughed a little strangled laugh, like he was choking. Only Emil saw his eyes, red and watery.

"I'm not ashamed to say it," Johann whispered. "I want my mother."

Emil laughed. "Me too, Johann. Me too."

Georg and Friedrich sidled up beside them. Emil and Johann exchanged a worried glance. *They didn't just hear them talking about wanting their mothers, did they?* If they had, Emil and Johann would never live it down.

"Well, boys," Friedrich said, toasting them with his beer. "Tomorrow we will be men."

Emil and Johann let out a breath.

"If sitting for endless hours on a less than luxurious train ride to our next stop, which will not be the front, makes us men," said Georg.

"But then we will fight," said Friedrich.

"No, then we will wait. Believe me," Georg continued, "we'll see more boredom than action for a long time."

"How do you know so much?" Emil said, shaking his head.

Georg took a long drag of his cigarette. "I watch. I listen. I read between the lines."

It crossed Emil's mind that Georg may have been recruited by the Gestapo. He and Johann had to be careful what they said around him, and that included more than talk about missing their mothers.

Georg and Friedrich drank freely and when they walked back to their bunkers, they had their arms around each other, singing old folk songs, each keeping the other from falling flat on his face.

Emil planned to stay far away from them the next morning.

He and Johann had to help them up onto their bunks.

"Come, on, Georg," Johann said. "You can do it."

Friedrich flopped over on his stomach, his arm pinned underneath. Emil couldn't stop a smug grin when he thought about how much that was going to hurt when he woke up.

Before Emil could get under his covers, there was a knuckle rap on the door. He opened it and a courier handed him an envelope. His mind went immediately to Father. Please, let him be okay. He opened the wire transcript.

ONKEL RUDI DIED STOP PLANE SHOT DOWN IN RUSSIA STOP LOVE MOTHER

Emil wondered why his mother thought it important enough for Emil to know about Onkel Rudi that she would bother to send a telegram? He felt bad for him, sure, but it's not like they were close. He'd only met the man a few times in his life, and most recently here in Nuremberg.

Was it a message? A sign? Her way of telling him that the war would not end in Germany's favor as Onkel Rudi believed and to try really hard in the meantime not to get killed?

His mother didn't know he was about to leave to fight on the front. At least Emil hadn't told her. He didn't want to worry her more, with Father fighting as well.

The next day, they were on a train. And Georg was right again: dirty, hard benches, windows so smudged with grime they could barely see out, cold, no luxuries, long and boring.

They passed the time by talking about girls, ammunition, and home, but then they just got homesick and everyone grew quiet. They nibbled on their rations, not wanting them to run out, since they didn't know when the next meal would be.

Every once in a while the train would stop to load up another unit of men. Usually it was a mix of fresh frecklyfaced boys and leathery wrinkled senior citizens. They'd have a few minutes to stand up and walk around.

Eventually they stopped in a small town with one insignificant church steeple silhouetted in the near darkness of dusk. Disembarking the train, they followed their commander, walking noiselessly like a family of rats through a ghost town.

Where did all the inhabitants go? Emil wondered.

Except for the odd call of distant wildlife, it was eerily quiet. No one dared to speak.

Finally, they reached the church. The pews had been removed, probably to burn for heat over the winter. The commander lit a candle; its glow bounced off the stained glass, reflecting eerie shades of red and blue.

They were instructed to bed down on the ground. Emil and Johann found a spot, laid out their bedrolls and tried to make themselves comfortable. Emil fell asleep in an instant.

A couple hours later he awoke, his body stinging. He scratched. The fire in his skin flared more. And he wasn't alone. Others had joined him in the battle of the itch.

"What is it?" Emil said.

"Fleas," said Johann. "Try to ignore them. We need our sleep."

In the morning, the regiment looked worse than they had the night before. No one had gotten any sleep. After a small breakfast of toast and barley coffee, they got back on the train, still hungry.

Emil noticed the train had three empty flat-decks on the front.

"That's in case the partisans planted land mines on the track. The flat-decks blow up, not us," Georg said.

"What's a partisan?" Emil said, scratching.

"A partisan is a member of an irregular army, one that opposes occupational rule."

Emil frowned. "An irregular army?"

"Yes. When we fight the Reds, we'll know who they are by their uniforms and their battle formations." He looked around to make sure everyone was listening. "But partisans, see, they're sneaky. They look like civilians, and they track you like animals, sneaking up on you from a ditch or a bush. Then, '*POW*'!" He slapped his hands together. "You're dead. You have to watch your back."

Great, another thing to be nervous and worried about, Emil thought. *Thanks, Georg.*

Emil rubbed a spot clean on the window. A vast plain of bare earth brushed with snow, stretched out as far as the eye could see. Occasionally, they'd pass a village, but Emil never saw any people.

After a number of days on the train, they landed in a small town in Ukraine, and set up barracks in an abandoned village. After four years of war, the paint had peeled off the walls and the yards and gardens had overgrown. Faded flower boxes beneath the windows were empty.

Rations waited for them, so at least they had a decent meal, and for the first time in weeks. They ate like kings at a feast–shaved ham, potatoes, cabbage. They could go to bed with a full stomach.

Afterward, Friedrich walked in with a bag of white powder. Along with fleas, they all had lice.

"That stinks!" Emil said. He was joined by a chorus of groans.

"It's insect powder," Friedrich said, sprinkling it over them. "It was developed by Dr. Theo Morell, the *Fuehrer*'s own personal physician."

How thoughtful of him, Emil thought. He could put up with the stench if it actually worked, but it didn't. Everyone was all the more cranky the next morning, for not only were they still itchy, they stank.

The fact that they didn't have a proper cleaning facility or clean clothes didn't help the matter. Bad smells came with war.

Emil put on his helmet, boots, and uniform. It was his turn to do guard duty. He stuck a small collapsible shovel in his belt, then strapped on a Mauser rifle. He turned to Johann.

"So, how do I look?"

"Like you're ready for the opera."

Johann was polishing his boots with a small brush that made soft *swish* sounds.

"Are you scared?" Emil prodded.

"Yes."

Emil shifted under the weight of the gun. "We are going to have to kill people."

Swish, swish. "Maybe."

"Johann, there is no getting around it, now."

Swish, swish, swish.

"Johann."

Johann threw his boot to the floor. "What do you want me to say, Emil? You know how I feel."

Emil hushed him, glancing over his shoulder. "Shh, I know. I'm sorry. We have to keep our voices down."

Johann whispered, pleading. "Please. I can't think about it right now."

"Okay, okay." Emil held his hand up. "Let's not talk about it anymore today."

He ran outside fearing repercussions if he were to be late for his post. He spotted Georg and a tall dark haired boy standing alongside the lieutenant and sighed.

"Come on, Radle," Georg said with a nod of his head. Apparently the lieutenant had informed him of where they were to stand guard, on the edge of the town near the main road they had come in on.

Georg took his command seriously, standing stout and still like a statue. Emil mimicked Georg's posture, ignoring the growing pain in his lower back and the pinch in his shoulder from the weight of his rifle. If Georg could do it than he could too.

The other boy's name was Joseph and he looked as incompetent and inexperienced as Emil felt. Reluctantly, Emil admitted to himself that Georg's take charge presence comforted him.

Sweat began to trickle down Emil's forehead, catching in his eyebrows before dripping into his eyes. He swiped his face with the back of his coat sleeve, desperate to strip himself of the senseless jacket in the growing summer heat. He glanced at Georg, stoic, with barely a shimmer of sweat on his brow. Emil frowned and wondered if his fellow soldier was even human.

Suddenly, Georg dropped to the ground and for a fleeting moment, Emil thought he might've fainted, and pushed back a feeling of delight at that thought.

Then Georg spat, "Get down, idiots!"

That's when Emil a dark shadow move through the trees in the forest beyond. He was on the ground beside Georg before he could breathe out his next breath, his heart racing.

"What is it?" Emil said. Probably just a deer.

"Partisans." Georg let off a shot and it echoed between them. Adrenalin laced fear shot through Emil's body as he cocked his own rifle. A shot was returned, and Emil flinched. He felt Joseph shake with nerves beside him.

Georg shot again, then threw them a sideways glare. "Shoot!"

Emil shot aimlessly, forcing himself to keep his eyes open, wishing they were better hidden than just laying flat on the ground. He continued to fire along with Georg and Joseph, hoping their shots would warn the partisans away, and give them an opportunity to get better cover and to retreat.

More shots rang out overhead. They sounded like they had come from behind. Emil risked a look over his shoulder. His company had heard the fighting and several soldiers were creeping in behind them. Emil's eyes settled back on the trees. A partisan screamed out as he fell to the forest floor.

Then it was over. An eerie quiet fell. Emil felt deafened by the sounds of gunfire that still rang in his ears and the blaring roar of his own breath in his ears. Once his heart began to slow he dared to look around him. Georg was on his knees, his brow furrowed as he assessed the situation. Joseph lay on his stomach and didn't budge. Emil prodded the boy's shoulder as bitter dread filled his heart. A patch of red blended in with the boy's dark hair. Emil pushed him over onto his back. Josef's eyes were open and turned upward, and a dark bullet hole marked his forehead.

Emil scuttled backwards, pushing back at the urge to vomit.

Chapter Thirty-Eight

Their company had recently joined two others, and Emil felt comforted by the swell of men, now numbering over eight hundred. They were like a small town, and perhaps there would be a way to get lost in the midst, that he and Johann could survive.

Because he now knew what Georg had known all along. The war didn't start on the front. It was being waged every step of the way there. Emil had thought his enemy would be a clearly marked Russian soldier, but it was in fact more insidious. He couldn't get Josef's blanched and lifeless face from his mind, or how Georg had removed his identification tags while reciting, "Fallen like a hero on the field of honor for Germany and the Fuehrer."

Their commander had received word a day ago that the crumbling line in the front was in dire need of supplies, especially food, and soldier re-enforcements and that they had to make haste.

Examined another way, Emil thought, it meant that the soldiers on the front were dying in battle and starving while doing so.

There weren't enough trucks to carry every soldier and most of the vehicles were loaded up with supplies for the front. The partisans didn't want these supplies to get there. They wanted them for themselves. Soldiers on guard duty stood atop the moving vehicles, scouting the areas before and around their troops. The men on the outside and behind also had field glasses to face and rifles ready.

The soberness of their assignment felt so incongruent with the day which was full of sunshine and blue skies. Birds could be heard chirping in the nearby forests. Emil tilted his face toward the sun allowing himself to forget where he was for just a moment.

A fellow soldier spotted his slight smile.

"Don't be fooled by the beauty of the day," he said. "The blue skies belong to the Russians."

Emil shot a look of questioning.

The soldier looked to be in his late twenties, with a sharp penetrating gaze. The frown lines on his face were deeply etched. "The Luftwaffe is nearly crippled," he continued. "If you hear aircraft engines, take cover."

Emil nodded. It sounded like good advice.

"I'm Philip, by the way," the soldier said. "I've been with this company for three years. I'm sorry to see you here and so young."

He said this with a deepening frown, and Emil figured Philip didn't expect him to survive his first battle.

If they ever got to it. The front was like a mirage in the desert; the more you walked toward it the farther it seemed to be. Emil's calves ached with all the walking and the strap of the Mauser rifle dug into his shoulder. He shifted over, closer to his neck for relief, but the weight of the weapon pulled it back into the raw groove.

To top it off, his boots bit into his ankles with every step, thumb sized blisters burst and burning with the sweat that dampened his socks. Emil was miserable with itchy sweat in the summer heat. All of the men were. Sweat dripped between his shoulder blades under his tunic and in the crevices of his underarms, under his chin and along the rim of his cap. He longed to gulp the remainder of the water in his canteen, but it was precariously empty and he had to preserve what he had until the next stop.

Emil scoured the faces looking for Johann. It was easy to get separated and Emil felt nervous when he lost sight of his only real friend. Then he spotted him marching beside Friedrich who was head and shoulders taller than most of the men and hard to miss.

They set up camp in another deserted town. Emil wondered where all the people had gone, but didn't blame them for wanting to get out of the way, especially when the town was crouched close to where the front line battle was brewing.

Emil noticed the banter decreased as each day progressed. Fatigue and nagging fear wore on a man's spirit along with his physical body. Johann hadn't spoken a word in days and though Emil tried to marked it up as normal under the circumstances, he worried about him.

The camp cook worked a miracle with few supplies, and Emil devoured the cup of stew and two hard buns provided to each man in minutes. He wasn't alone. The space around him filled with the sounds of metal spoon scraping every last drop of gravy from the tin cups.

The weather had cooled a little and he reclined on his pack in the grass allowing himself to feel a small measure of contentedness. Johann did the same.

"I can't stop thinking of home," he said.

"Me neither," Emil admitted, silently adding "or Katharina."

"I still can't believe we're in the middle of this nightmare," Johann continued, his voice catching. Emil hoped he wasn't about to cry.

"It will be over soon," Emil said. "Just take it a day at a time. Eventually it will end."

Then Emil heard a sound that made his blood curdle. The hum of an Aircraft engine. He remembered what Philip had told him.

"Quick, Johann!" he said, crouching, preparing to take flight. But where to? Not to one of the vehicles. A strike to one of them would blow them up, too.

Everyone heard the engines now, and mayhem erupted as men grabbed their weapons, many running for cover in the church. Emil sprinted for the nearest cottage and kicked at the wooden door with his foot. Visions of Helmut and Karl lying in the field after their strafing attack shot flashed through Emil's mind. They had to get out of sight. Pure panic squeezed his chest tight.

"Help," he shouted to Johann. But they were too late. A single plane flew overhead. It was one of theirs, a straggler.

Emil fell to the ground in a heap, near to tears with relief.

Pure exhaustion brought on a dreamless sleep that night despite the heat and mosquitoes, but Emil awoke to the sounds of men scratching and cursing.

The next day produced more marching in the heat. Emil was assigned to guard duty for the morning near the front of the troop. The road beneath them was uneven dark dry soil riddled with rocks. Each step produced a cloud of dust and more than one man stumbled when their toes inadvertently hit a stone.

Though alert to his situation and the fellow soldiers with rifles ready around him, Emil found distraction from the tediousness and raw ache of marching by letting his mind wander to kinder times. Images of his mother and father, fatter and happy, Helmut playing in a carefree world of make-believe. He pushed back memories that included his bad behavior toward them.

Or of the food his mother used to prepare, like roast ham and dumplings. Chocolate torte.

Emil's stomach growled in response. He took a sip of water and mentally reprimanded himself for the self-torture.

Instead he let his mind drift to Katharina and their kiss good-bye. Her blue eyes desperate for him to stay, the tight clasp of her hand in his.

The blue string. A promise that she would be there when he returned.

The reason why he must return.

They marched along the dry road that narrowed to almost a goat path. The vehicles lurched along single file, along the twists and turns, all of the soldiers on guard as if something was bound to dart out of the trees.

Then something did. Dark and low to the ground, it raced across the path in the distance. The commanding officer ordered the convoy to halt. The soldier beside Emil shot at the moving target, but missed.

Before Emil's mind could registered that the black spot moved too quickly for a partisan, it burst out of the trees onto the road. Emil shot involuntarily, joining the cacophony of rifle fire around him.

The spot dropped to the ground. The officer waved to one of the soldiers to investigate. Half way to the corpse, our soldier started hooting with something close to laughter.

"A wild boar!" he shouted.

A wild boar! News of the kill flew among the ranks, and a cheer rose to heaven. Emil wasn't alone in dreaming about the roast dinner to come.

Before too long, the animal was tied by the ankles and strapped to the back of one of the trucks. The mood of the men cheered considerably.

Their guard down as they entered the vacant village around the bend.

Shots rang out again and several men collapsed to the dirt near Emil, including the soldier that had just minutes before rejoiced with the announcement of the boar. A chorus of "Ambush!" filled the air, as the men took cover behind the vehicles, in the ditches and behind brush.

Emil fell to the earth with only dead bodies as his cover. His heart beat madly against his ribs. He shot randomly over the nearest corpse.

The Spandau machine guns were engaged. Grenades thrown and shot into the village huts. Huts burst into flames, and partisans ran to the woods.

Their lieutenant shouted for them to pursue. Emil scrambled to his feet and ran. He felt exposed, like he was chasing shadows.

Ahead of him a partisan jumped from the tall grass and sprinted like a wild animal. Emil aimed, but hesitated. He could kill a fleeing target.

But this one was different. This one was a woman.

A woman partisan? Had the war come to this?

Emil lowered his rifle but heard a shot resound anyway. The woman screamed, falling. Another comrade had no such qualms about killing her.

The partisans weren't unskilled in guerilla warfare. They'd hidden bombs in the ground. The soldier running ahead of Emil tripped a wire. The blast of the bomb shook the earth as the man's body was shredded and fell to the ground. Pieces of his flesh splattered on Emil's arms and he thrust it about like his jacket was on fire.

German soldiers dropped like flies around him, and Emil felt his pant leg grow warm with urine as he scrambled away, looking for safety. He found it in a root hole and stayed positioned there, praying that Johann had somehow remained in one piece.

He waited until he heard the familiar sound of the lieutenant's whistle. The battle had ended.

Though they had killed most of the partisans who had attacked them, they lost seventy men and two supply trucks doing it. The partisans were devoted to stopping the convoy of supplies from reaching the Germans on the front and the boar had been a ploy of distraction.

The beast was roasted up as planned, but there was no accompanying happy celebration.

Chapter Thirty-Nine

Three days after the partisan attack they finally arrived to the front. It was a place called Ternopil, a muddy barren wasteland. A summer storm pelted rain on Emil's face like sharp grains of sand, the wind whipping through his uniform. He spit black dirt moving it out with his tongue. Emil couldn't fathom why they were fighting over this desolate piece of landscape.

He didn't have time to think about that now. They'd barely arrived before being thrown into the fray like mice dumped into a pit of snakes.

Ahead were three rows of hills behind which hid an incredible number of Soviets. Soviets who were not untrained with subpar ammunition like the partisans, but who had machine guns, tanks, and trucks mounted with rocket launchers. Emil's unit had those things too, but not in the same numbers. And worst of all, the Soviets had airplanes. The *Luftwaffe*, Emil's beloved *Luftwaffe*, had been all but destroyed.

Deafening, head throbbing explosions went off to Emil's left. Then right. Now straight ahead. He ducked and dodged, shooting off his newly issued machine gun, *rat-a-tat-tat*, through the haze, praying that he didn't hit one of his own.

Johann, Friedrich and Georg, who had also managed to survive the partisan attack, were doing the same. At times they ducked behind tankers, and other times fell flat on the ground. Their faces were twisted in shock, flushed red with panic. Emil's body felt like it moved outside the will of his own mind. With an animal-like instinct, he scampered and crawled, his eyes watering and filling with dust, caking like mud.

Their squadron crawled forward bravely, bit by bit, shooting rockets from their tanks. Though they were powerful and intimidating, kicking up dust that blind Emil while shattering his eardrums, they were yet noticeably inferior to the Reds.

A Russian rocket exploded to Emil's left, knocking him to the ground. He grabbed at his ear, which rang painfully.

"Get up!" Johann grabbed him by the arm and they moved on, stepping over bodies, German and Russian, as they went.

They continued forward when everything in their hearts, minds and bodies demanded they turn and run the other way. But, if they did that, they'd be dead for sure, shot by their own men.

The barrenness of the land left them exposed, vulnerable, easy targets for the Reds. They covered themselves by sticking close to the tanks, hiding behind the odd tree or worse, a dead body.

Emil's heart raced like a scared rodent's, his lungs gasping air in short puffs. His stomach churned, turning his bowels to liquid. He couldn't imagine surviving this endless, hellish day. But he had to. If he died, it would crush his mother and break Katharina's heart.

Up ahead, Emil spotted a scarce bush. He and Johann collapsed behind it, exhausted.

Emil pulled out his shovel and started digging a foxhole. Johann joined him, digging to save their lives.

"I don't even want to fight this stupid war!" Johann said with bitterness.

"Shut, up!" Emil snapped. His nerves were shot, and his patience along with it. Maybe Johann didn't care if he were shot down by one of their own commanders for treason. Emil wanted to live.

"Stop whining like a baby." Georg had come from nowhere, out of the shadows. Emil was afraid he might turn his gun on Johann. Instead he started digging.

"We have to kill these imbeciles. Don't you know what they do to their POWs?"

Johann ran his sleeve under his nose. "They can't do much to me if I'm dead."

"You are such an infant, Johann," George said loudly. "So, you're dead. But what about your family. You got a mother? A sister?"

Johann shrugged. Emil didn't like where this was going. A bomb dropped, they all flinched.

"You know what they do to German women and girls?" Georg shouted above the noise. "They rip their clothes off and rape them. Take turns. While their men are holding the lanterns so they can see and hear everything. Then the Reds shoot them. The women first, then the men."

It was no secret the Reds hated them. Really, really hated them. Emil believed him.

"Johann," Emil said. "We have to fight. For our mothers. For Katharina."

Johann slumped to the bottom of their fox hole and covered his face with his hands. Emil was afraid Johann was about to start bawling, proving Georg right in his

228

accusations. But he didn't. He took a deep breath and said, "I'm fighting already, aren't I?"

Each day when darkness began to fall, Emil was filled with wonder that they were still alive to live another day.

But before they could collapse into their hard, dirty beds and wish for sleep void of nightmares they still had to load up the dead. The injured were transported to the mobile hospitals several kilometers away from the front.

There was no getting used to it. Emil grabbed the arms of one corpse as Johann took the legs, both of them trying to ignore the ripped flesh, crushed limbs and stinking wounds.

One dead body after another.

The next morning, a low fog sifted through the camp. Emil could barely see his hand in front of his face.

"We're retreating," Georg said when he joined them. The normal cockiness of his tone, gone. He'd shrunk into a sliver of a man, seemingly overnight. He was just a boy.

They all looked like that, Emil thought. Stick men. Sick, stupid stick men.

The squadron packed up the barracks, and walked west to the next village. Emil struggled with the weight of his kit, fearful about how frail he had gotten. Each step was a monumental effort. Though several hundred men remained, the trip was quiet. No unnecessary talking was permitted or desired.

They finally settled on the least deplorable looking abandoned building and set up shop. Emil and Friedrich scoured the village for anything wooden, anything that could be broken up and burned.

"Why don't you like me, Emil?"

Emil looked at Friedrich sharply, not certain where that had come from. He had heard that crisis situations had a way of making people closer, and to his surprise Emil felt a certain fondness for Friedrich now.

"What do you mean, Friedrich?"

Friedrich's head was down, his eyes scouring the earth and avoiding Emil's gaze. "I know we haven't always, you know, been the best of friends."

Was he trying to apologize?

"I like you," Emil said. He did a little bit, now, so it wasn't a complete untruth.

Friedrich paused. Emil could see his large Adam's apple go up and down, struggling to swallow. His voice cracked. "If I don't make it, you'll tell my mother, you know, I'm sorry."

Run and duck, run and duck. Explosions on all sides and from the air. Heart beating, quicker, faster. Sweat dripping from his brow into his eyes. This wasn't a dream. This was real. In his constant state of fear and fatigue, Emil couldn't tell the difference anymore. When did he wake and how did he get here? Every moment was a blur.

With his peripheral, Emil saw Johann, his face stiff, eyebrows arched in panic, dread. Another fierce explosion and they dropped to the ground. Emil braced his machine gun against his shoulder and pulled the trigger. He didn't even open his eyes.

A panzer rolled by, and Emil and Johann jumped up to run alongside it, hoping it would provide some cover, some protection from the ferocious attack of the Red Army, stronger now than any other day.

Emil heard a man scream. The noise around him was overwhelming, all-consuming, but he heard it. He turned and saw Johann on the ground, writhing. Writhing and screaming. His leg was gone.

"Johann!" Emil ran to him, pulled off his belt and strapped it around Johann's stump, pulling it tight. He couldn't help it, he turned away and vomited.

Sucking in his sour breath, he grabbed Johann under his arms and dragged his wailing friend back, away from the enemy line.

Bombs dropped from over head, bullets whizzing. Emil kept dragging Johann, back-step, slide. His screams became moans. Almost there. Medical truck in sight.

Burning heat in his right leg. Emil gasped, dropping Johann's heavy body. He was hit. A bullet. Emil fell with a thud, Johann falling against him. Friedrich caught up to them from behind, pausing briefly to register—two soldiers down.

"Those dirty dogs!" Friedrich's face contorted, devil-like. His long legs sprinted towards the front; he hollered a deep belly yell, *For the Fatherland!* shooting his machine gun with wild madness.

The shots were returned. Friedrich's body shuddered as it was riddled with bullets. He slumped to the ground in a pool of blood.

Emil jerked himself backwards, one painful pull at a time, trying to hang on to Johann as he went. More pain.

Vicious, searing, tearing pain. Another hit—his shoulder this time, blood spurting.

Then blackness.

Chapter Forty

His eyelids felt like lead blankets. His lips like frayed ropes. A moan escaped through them when he shifted his weight—pain burst through his entire right side.

Where was he?

He worked his eyelids open a crack, then closed them quickly. Bright light, blinding, singed his eyes.

An itch in his throat, a dry cough.

"Emil?" A voice. Familiar. His brain raced to place it, but drew a blank.

Whoever it was slipped a straw in between his lips. He sucked back cool water. Eagerly. Too eagerly. He gagged.

"Easy," the voice said. "There's more where this came from."

He attempted to open his eyes again. Images blurred against the light. Someone leaned over him.

A girl?

He must be dreaming. This whole thing must be a dream. He hadn't seen a girl in months.

Especially not this girl. She looked like Irmgard.

A bad dream. He told himself to go back to sleep.

"Emil?" The girl nudged his left arm. "Are you awake?"

"Irmgard?"

"Yes, it's me! Isn't this amazing? I'm an auxiliary nurse. I couldn't believe it when they brought you and Johann in."

Johann. He was with him out on the front line. He remembered now. Friedrich crumbling like a used rag to the ground. Johann screaming. His bloody stump.

"Johann! Is he okay?" Emil tried to sit up. Bad move. The pain screamed once again.

"Shh," Irmgard said. "Stay still. Johann is here, in the bed next to you."

More carefully this time, Emil turned his head to the right. His friend was there, sleeping. Head wrapped. The new form of his body obvious under the white sheet: one leg, one stump.

"He's lucky I was here," she said.

"What do you mean?"

"We don't usually bother attending to wounds if it's clear the soldier is no longer able to go back on the field."

"You just let them die?"

"So many wounded come in every day. But because I was here, I told them I knew him. That he was fighting in the same unit as my brother."

"But Rolf isn't in our unit."

She winked. "I know."

"Why would they care what you said? It's not like you're a general in the army."

"No" she said, with a sly grin. "But I know one." She pulled apart her cardigan, smoothing her hand over her skirt, over a barely hidden bump. She was expecting a child.

"I didn't know you were married."

"Oh, I'm not." She covered her grin with her hand. "This is for the *Fuehrer*. We need new sons to lead the thousand-year Reich."

Was she serious? She was stupider than Georg.

"You know," she bent over to whisper. "I used to have a crush on you."

"Oh?"

"How could you not know?" she seemed surprised. "Hey, why didn't you like me?"

Emil wanted to stay on her good side. He couldn't tell her he thought she was a psychotic bigot.

"Um, I did like you. I just, you know, wasn't sure, uh, what to do about girls back then."

"Boys can be so simple minded." she sighed "But you know, I still think you're pretty good-looking." She stood to go. "Maybe, after the war, we can..." she patted her stomach and winked. "You know, make good for the Fatherland."

Emil sighed. He dreaded the day he'd have to tell Johann that he had Irmgard to thank for saving his life.

Chapter Forty-One

Emil had been lucky. The bullet to his shoulder was just a flesh wound, and looked more like a bad whipping than a gun shot. The bullet to his leg had missed the bone and major arteries. There was muscle and nerve damage, and his gait had been forever altered, but at least he was walking again.

He spent the cold month of November in the field hospital where he had decent food, warmth, and relative safety. In his mind, it was worth a bullet to get away from the horrors of fighting on the front.

Though his injuries were serious enough to keep him away from that hell, they weren't bad enough to grant him a trip home. Instead they shipped him back to Nuremberg.

Because the war wasn't over.

Even though everyone knew that they had already lost it.

Of course, Johann was shipped back to Passau. Emil was certain the stump would heal; he was more concerned for his friend's spirit.

"I wish I'd died on that field," Johann whispered one night. "Why didn't you leave me? Why didn't you just let me die?"

Emil whispered back, "Would you've left me?"

It was early December when they shipped him back to Nuremberg on a grimy, over-full train. He limped around the base with his crutches pinching his underarms, wondering how he could be of much use around there.

A new boy was sitting upright on the lone wooden chair in the room when Emil shuffled in.

"*Hallo,*" Emil said.

"*Grüss Gott.*"

"My name's Emil. Who are you?"

"I am Günther."

Like everyone else Emil knew, Günther looked as if he hadn't eaten much lately. He was small, his skin a ghostly white. Emil guessed that he wasn't much older than his own brother Helmut.

Günther hadn't claimed one of the upper bunks, like Georg and Friedrich had when they had first arrived, and since Emil was unable to climb to a top bunk, he was forced to take the lower one next to Günther. They were so close they could touch each other in the night.

"Do you want to take an upper bunk?" Emil said. "It's okay with me."

"I'd rather not, if you don't mind." Günther laced his fingers together, staring hard at them.

He was the polar opposite of Georg, Emil thought as he studied his new roommate. Where Georg was strong and dominating, Günther seemed frail and shy. Where Georg liked to command all conversation, Günther was reluctant to speak.

Emil wondered what had happened to Georg? Had he fallen, or was he still alive somewhere?

SS Officer Spiegl had moved to a new post. Albert Jäger was the new commander of the Nuremberg training camp.

Emil couldn't believe it. "Jäger?"

"That's Officer Jäger, to you, Radle!"

Damn.

Albert Jäger strutted around like a pompous king. He was a taller, thinner version of his father, and not that much older than Emil. Emil hated taking orders from him.

"I'll be watching you," Jäger said, "I know about that traitor, that friend of yours."

Emil's hands formed tight fists by his side. *Leave Moritz out of it.*

"My father's keeping an eye on your mother and brother, too. There's something not right there."

"You watch it," Emil said.

"No, you watch it, Radle." He snapped his heels together and saluted. "*Heil Hitler!*"

"*Heil Hitler,*" Emil answered, hating him for forcing a show of loyalty. Albert Jäger held his gaze as they both held their salute, and Emil dared not look away first. Then Albert spun on his heels, leaving Emil to shoot daggers in his back with his glare.

Time skidded to a near halt, the days stretching out before Emil with excruciating slowness. They did drills over and over again until Emil felt he could do them in his sleep. In fact he often dreamed about the drills, never able to get away from his captivity at the base. His mind tortured him with homesickness. The memory of a kitchen filled with his family and the heavenly smell of fresh bread.

And thoughts of Katharina. Always Katharina.

It seemed his only task was to wait and wait some more. Wait for the war to return to Nuremberg.

One morning there was a knock on the bunk door, which was odd, since no one ever "visited" in the morning. Emil opened the door and Hans, whom Emil recognized from the base, walked in with his personal bag in hand.

"Sorry to intrude," he said, "but I'm your new bunkmate." With that declaration he made claim to the free bunk above Günther.

"I don't understand," Emil said. "What's wrong with your own bunker?"

"They didn't explain. I'm just following orders."

Emil shook his head. He hadn't seen any new boys around, no new arrivals.

After a short breakfast of oatmeal and boiled eggs, Albert made a show of marching to the front of the room. He straightened his lapels before making an announcement.

"As you all are well aware, our great nation is at a critical hour." Albert clasped his hands behind his back, his eyes darting to the side door. He continued, "Extreme circumstances call for extreme measures and in the time of war it becomes necessary to employ all resources in order to stay the course and gain victory."

Emil's stomach flipped. He clenched his mid-section, nervously waiting for Albert to make his pronouncement. *What was it this time, a return to the front? In Russia, perhaps?*

"So, to that end, I would like to introduce you to our new recruits."

And in walked a group of girls.

The boys gasped. Emil recalled the female partisan shot down in front of him and frowned. Hitler had conscripted girls to fight his war. It had come to that for the German army now.

They wore trousers. Besides the partisan, Emil had never seen a lady in trousers before; he didn't think any of the other boys there had either. They all had their hair braided and tied up.

Their chaperone instructed them to line up against the wall. Emil groaned. The fourth one from the end. She lifted her chin and turned her face towards Emil. She found his eyes and offered a soft smile.

Katharina.

Albert cleared his throat. "I'll leave you to get acquainted for a few minutes before the training session begins."

Hans grinned and started chuckling. "Thank you, Hitler," he said and walked toward the small group of girls. He wasn't alone. With the exception of Günther, all the boys sauntered over, looking to make a good first impression.

Emil was amazed at how fast his bad leg could go when he was motivated to move. In an instant he was standing before her.

He grabbed her wrist and pulled her away from the crowd. "What are you doing here?" he demanded.

The sparkle in her eyes dimmed. "You're not happy to see me?"

"No, I'm not!"

Her jaw tightened as she turned her face from him.

"It's not that," Emil said, longing to pull her close. "I am happy to see you. Just not here. Not like this. It's not safe."

"I'm sorry. I didn't have a choice."

Emil regretted his harshness. Of course she hadn't chosen to come. And if she was to be conscripted, he wanted her with him. He was thankful Passau fell into the Nuremberg jurisdiction.

He let out a long, slow breath and said, "I'm sorry. Can we start again?"

Katharina nodded.

Emil wanted to kiss her, but he didn't dare in front of the others He shook her hand and didn't let go. "Welcome to Nuremberg."

"Thank you. It's a pleasure to be here." She smiled, sharing his joke.

"Who's that?" she said, looking over his shoulder.

Emil turned around. Günther was there, hovering.

"That's my shadow, Günther."

"Introduce me."

Emil called him over. "Günther, meet my, uh, good friend, Katharina. She's also from Passau."

Günther tentatively shook her hand.

"There's Fraulein Hanenberg," Katharina said, after a moment. "She's our officer. I have to go." She squeezed Emil's hand again before leaving. "I'll see you later."

That evening Emil took Katharina on a tour of Nuremberg. He was used to seeing bombed out buildings, and holes in the ground filled with rubble, but Katharina hadn't seen anything like it yet.

Her eyes were bright with horror. "This is terrible."

In the light of early dusk, the broken buildings stared down on them like wounded giants; half their large bodies ripped away, their eyes dark squares of broken glass.

"Not all of Nuremberg is destroyed," Emil said. "There are still a few streets that remain fairly normal." They turned down one of them and passed by the pub where some of the other recruits were hanging out. Hans spotted them and motioned for them to join.

Emil tapped the small of her back. "Do you want to go in?"

"For a little while, just to warm up."

It was a small, smoky room, with dark wood beams and exposed brick. Albert was there, and Emil almost spun around and left. But Katharina was cold so they sat at a table across from each other and ordered coffee.

"As much as I hate that you're here," Emil said, "it is so great to be with you again."

"I know," she said. "I moped around for days after you left. My mother threatened to tie me up."

"How is he, how is Johann?"

Katharina let her gaze drift to the window. "I don't know. He's alive on the outside, but on the inside...I can't find him. He was furious when he found out I was being sent here but relieved that at least I would be with you."

She looked back at Emil. "How are you? Does your leg hurt you terribly?"

He'd grown accustomed to the chronic pain, and didn't want to burden Katharina unnecessarily. He shook his head. "Not much."

She lifted her cup to her lips and Emil saw the blue thread around her finger. He hadn't noticed it before, and felt glad that she had left it on. He remembered their time together in the park, how he professed his love, lost himself in her kisses.

When she put her cup down, Emil grabbed her hand. "So, we're still engaged," he said, grinning, wanting to change the mood of their conversation.

"Of course!" she smiled. "You didn't think you could get rid of me that easily, did you Emil?"

"I never want to get rid of you."

He'd held her hand for too long. Hans and his buddy, Franz, strolled over. "Hi lovebirds," Hans said squishing in beside Katharina. Emil felt himself go red and hoped Hans hadn't embarrassed Katharina. "Mind if we join you?"

Not that Emil could have refused him. Franz pushed in next to him. He and Hans drank beer; Hans tipped his glass and took a swig.

"You're an old pro," he said looking at Emil. "How long until we see some action around here?"

"What kind of action are you talking about?" said Franz, winking.

Hans elbowed Katharina. "I don't know. What kind of action am I talking about, sweetheart?"

"Hey!" Emil said. His hands curled into fists.

"Excuse me," Katharina said. "I think we should go."

"No, no, I'm just kidding," Hans said. "Relax. Emil, come on, you know what kind of action I mean."

"How am I supposed to know," Emil said.

"I'm getting kind of bored," Hans said. "You know?"

"Me too," said Franz, who was a lot like Hans. In fact, Emil thought, he probably wished he were Hans.

"We'd be lucky to stay bored," Emil said through tight lips, his knuckles still white.

Hans turned to Katharina. "He's no fun, is he?"

"I'm warm enough," she said, ignoring Hans. "Let's go."

"Oh, come on," Hans groaned. "You don't really have to go."

"Actually, I do. I have a curfew and Fraulein Hanenberg will punish me if I'm late."

"Fine," he said, getting up to let Katharina out, touching her shoulder and her lower back as he did so. Emil felt like punching him in the face.

Albert watched them leave.

"Sorry about them," Emil said as they walked back to the base. "They had too much to drink."

She sighed. "Boys will be boys."

Emil dropped Katharina off at her bunker and this time he kissed her, long and lingering.

"Good night," he said."

"See you in the morning." She blew him a kiss as he walked away.

Günther was already in his bunk when he got back. Emil crept into bed, clothes on. He did this for two reasons. One, it was cold, and two he had learned from his last duty to always be ready for anything.

"I'm not sleeping," Günther said. "You don't have to be quiet because of me."

"I'm tired. I want to go to sleep now," Emil said. Then he grew curious. "What'd you do tonight?"

"Not much. I have some books. I read a bit," Günther said. "How about you?"

"I showed Katharina around Nuremberg."

"Is she your girl?"

"What do you mean?"

"Is she your girlfriend or just a girl you'd like to be your girlfriend?" Günther rolled onto his side. "I'd say she's already your girlfriend, or you plan on making it that way real soon."

Emil would've liked to tell Günther the truth, that Katharina was his girlfriend, fiancé, and so much more. That she meant everything to him and that he planned to marry her as soon as the war was over. But that kind of information loose in these barracks would just cause them trouble.

"That's the most I've ever heard you say at one time," Emil said instead. "When did you become a relationship expert?"

"I'm just good at observing people."

"I see." Emil turned over and faced the wall. "Then you should be able to tell what I'm doing now."

Chapter Forty-Two

E mil was gratified the next morning to see that Hans and Franz were looking a bit green and didn't have much of an appetite for breakfast. That meant there would be more for the rest of them, and that maybe it would shut them up for a while.

After breakfast, during Flak training, Albert called on him.

"Since apparently you are skilled and experienced on Flak, I would like you to instruct some of our new recruits. I'll send over two."

He recognized Katharina's gait as her silhouette broke through the sunlight. "Good morning," she said when she reached him.

It certainly has gotten better, Emil thought, smiling at her. A ginger haired girl followed behind. "I'm Bettina," she said, lowering her chin, her eyes wide and flirty.

Emil cleared his throat. "Well, let's get started." He ran his hand along the barrel of the gun. "This is an 88 millimeter heavy Flak gun. There are smaller versions of this out on the field. The first one I trained on in Passau was a small, one-man Flak."

The girls studied Emil. He took a quick breath and continued. "This Flak will fire altitude-fused shells up to fifteen meters, at three shells a minute. When used alongside searchlights, they can be quite deadly."

"Have you ever shot a plane down?" asked Katharina.

All the chatter and noise from the other units faded, and Emil felt like he and Katharina stood alone on the earth. Blood whooshed through his ears as she waited calmly for his confession. She'd been part of their small group of resisters. *We didn't believe in the war, remember?*

"I don't work alone," he answered. If Bettina was confused by his answer, Katharina wasn't.

"It's really very powerful, and very dangerous." Emil stared hard at her. "You shouldn't be here."

"But I am."

"I'm here, too!" Bettina butted in, frowning.

Emil shook his head and the world around him came back into focus. "I meant both of you."

Hans and Franz were doing drills on the next station and every time Albert was out of sight, they would make annoying catcalls to the girls.

"Hey, beauties! Why don't you come hang out with us real men?"

Emil felt blood rush to his face. He curled his fists.

"Just ignore them," Katharina said.

Bettina was distracted by the boys. And tempted. Before Emil could say anything she was over with Hans and Franz, giggling and fluttering her eyelashes.

Katharina ran a hand down the large Flak canon and then looked up into the sky.

"People were dying." Emil tried to explain. "Women and children. I had to shoot back to help save them."

"Do you think we're safe now? I mean all the military bases and factories near here have been hit already."

"It's not just about the bases and factories anymore." No, it was way more complicated than that. "Now they're out for blood."

The bell rang announcing lunch and everyone immediately headed back to the mess hall. Franz had his arm around Bettina. Hans sneaked up behind Emil and Katharina and scooped Katharina up in his arms, twirling her.

"Put me down!"

"Katharina, why do you insist on hanging out with that cripple, when you could have me?" Hans put her down and she pushed herself away just as Emil stepped in front of him. He clocked him in the nose.

"Hey!" Hans' hand went to his face. There was blood.

"You stay away from her!" Emil yelled.

"Or what?" He lunged at Emil throwing him to the ground.

They wrestled and for a moment Emil was on top. He punched Hans in the face again.

A crowd had gathered, but Emil couldn't tell who they were cheering on. He only knew that the pain in his leg was sapping his strength.

They rolled again and now Emil was on the bottom. He saw Hans pull his fist back and braced for impact. Then his head exploded. Emil's right eye felt like it burst and he knew it'd be black and swollen by the end of the day.

Franz pulled Hans off Emil before he could do more damage. "Enough!" he said. "If Jäger gets wind of this, we'll all be in for it."

Hans was breathing hard, too. His nose still bled as he shook himself off and left.

Emil's head pounded.

"Are you okay?" Katharina knelt on the ground beside him. He felt like an idiot. If you're going to start a fight, you better win it, and he definitely hadn't won this one.

"Yeah."

"Well, thanks, for, you know. Sticking up for me."

"Sure."

Albert would hear about their scrap, Emil was certain of it. How could he miss his black eye and Hans's bruised nose? Lucky for all of them, Albert just found it amusing.

The days fell into a pattern of breakfast, drill training, lunch, farm/base labor, the evening meal, with leisure time in the evenings, often spent at the pub. It was a change of scenery from the base, and a place to take refuge from the winter winds.

Emil's eye healed even if his ego didn't, but when Katharina looked at him, it was like she couldn't see the bruising of his eye, the limp of his leg, or any of his many flaws. They'd agreed early on to try to keep their relationship undercover, purposely sitting apart during meals and mingling with other soldiers in the evening.

But Emil knew he couldn't keep the admiration he felt for her hidden. His eyes gave him away.

He was sitting beside Günther on a bar stool at the pub. He tried to be polite and nodded when Günther spoke, which thankfully, wasn't very often, but mostly his eyes lingered over his left shoulder where Katharina sat with a couple of girls.

"Oh, just go to her, already," Günther sputtered.

"What?"

"You're driving me crazy with your puppy-dog eyes," he said. "Do us both a favor, okay."

Emil stared at Günther. "You feel strongly about this, I see."

Günther shrugged and chugged at his beer.

Emil pulled the scarf away from his neck. He had warmed up, and as he stood to cross the room, he felt heat surge through his chest.

The girls with Katharina spotted him first, stopping mid sentence to watch him limp his final step towards them, and pull a chair out beside Katharina.

"Evening, ladies," he said with a smile. "Do you mind if I join you?"

"We don't mind," a brunette said. "Do you mind, Katharina?"

Katharina smiled, and a rosy blush filled her cheeks. "No, I don't mind."

Emil turned his attention to Katharina's bunkmates, asking them where they were from, how their families were, clearly charming them.

At the same time he reached under the table and grabbed Katharina's hand, not letting go until the pub closed and it was time to leave.

That night they were awakened by the sirens.

Emil, Günther and Hans jumped out of bed, grabbed their helmets and ran out to the Flak stations. Emil searched the sky but couldn't see any signs of enemy aircraft. No muffled noise of propeller engines, no search lights.

"Where are they?" yelled Günther.

"I don't see anything." The sirens screamed as Albert barked out instructions over them. Katharina found Emil at the mound. She looked frightened and he wanted to hold her tight. Once again he burned with anger that she was here.

Albert commanded, "Ready yourselves, load canons...."

Emil still couldn't see anything. He grabbed a canon ball, stuffing it in the barrel of the gun, and fumbling for the fuse.

"And halt!" Albert's face stretched as he shouted. "It's just a test."

A test?

"Everyone, go back to bed." And with that, Albert marched away, leaving them standing in the cold.

The sirens stopped, and Emil felt slapped by the sudden silence. Katharina stood stiff, staring after Albert.

"He's a jerk," Emil said, then grabbed her by the shoulders. "Are you all right?"

"Yes, I'm fine," she said, but she was trembling. "I can do this, Emil. I have to."

They started walking, but somehow they didn't end up back at the bunkers. Katharina had looped an arm through Emil's and he was glad.

"It's Christmas Eve," she said.

"When?"

"Tonight."

"It is?" He hadn't been following. The war was the main attraction.

"Yes, it is."

They stood still, inches apart snowflakes dropping gently on their heads.

"Well, then," Emil said. "Merry Christmas."

She turned her face up, "Merry Christmas."

Emil leaned down and kissed her. Her sweet cool lips warmed his soul and he really hoped they had a future after the war.

The next day Albert called Emil over.

"There's no romance allowed on base. I'm moving your girlfriend to another Flak station."

"She's not my girlfriend." He'd deny anything to keep her with him.

"Really, Radle? Anyway, it doesn't matter. I've decided to move her. It's done."

"But, it's Christmas Day!" Emil hoped to appeal to Albert's good will, but it was to no avail.

"What do I care about Christmas? It means nothing to me."

Emil was furious with himself. He was the one who failed to be discreet with his feelings, and because of this, Katharina had been re-stationed at the Flak post to the north. They were too far away to speak to each other now, but at least when they were manning Flaks, he could still see her from a distance.

Chapter Forty-Three

1945
JANUARY

There wasn't anything official planned to celebrate the new year of 1945. Most of the senior officers went home to be with family while the younger soldiers were left to fend for themselves on the base.

It was Katharina's idea to throw a little party. At first there wasn't a lot of enthusiasm—the future was more ominous than ever, certainly nothing worth celebrating, but Katharina insisted. We're only young once, she'd said. Emil remembered thinking, that was true, and hoped the war would end soon and they'd actually get to grow old.

Katharina had roused up the girls, and though at first they begrudgingly assisted her with preparing food and decorating the mess hall, soon they grew excited.

Emil found a phonograph and records that had been stored away in a closet. Hans and Franz took up a collection and purchased several cases of beer from the pub before it closed.

Since there were more guys than girls, the ladies were kept busy dancing from fellow to fellow, but by midnight, the mood on the base was the highest it had ever been as far as Emil could remember. The hall was filled with cigarette smoke, chatter and laughter, and when the countdown began, they shouted together, "*Zehn, neun, acht...drei, zwei, ein, null!!*"

Emil embraced Katharina and kissed her. She laughed. "Nineteen forty-five is our year, Emil. Just wait and see. The war will end and then it will just be about us!"

They danced together—clumsy in their inexperience and falling behind beat with his weak leg—until the sky lightened, washing the dusty room with sunshine. When Emil finally fell on his bunk to sleep, he was the happiest he'd been in a long, long while.

Emil dared to dream about life after the war. It couldn't end well for the Germans, that had become blatantly clear, but it would end. *Then what? Could there be freedom again in some form?* Whatever happened, he'd be okay, as long as he had Katharina by his side.

His dreams turned into a nightmare.

Moritz is alive; it's Emil's wedding day. Katharina in a white dress, smiling at him.

Sirens. *At their wedding?*

Sirens. Piercing, screeching sirens. He popped upright in bed, his ears ringing. This was real.

He'd slept in his clothes. He always slept in his clothes.

Plunking his helmet on, he scrambled after the others, through moonless darkness to the Flak stations.

His mind was numb, but somewhere in its deep recesses he knew this wasn't a test. It was real this time.

He was right. First he heard the engines, then he saw the lights. Incoming enemy aircraft.

Hands shaking, breath heaving, they worked to load the Flak guns.

"And, ready!" Albert yelled.

Emil lit the fuse.

"Fire!"

The earth trembled. The thrust of the explosion nearly threw him over.

Though he couldn't see her in the moonless night, Emil knew Katharina was at her station, doing the same pattern as he. Loading the canons, lighting the fuses.

Bomb after bomb fell; the ground rumbled and waved ceaselessly—Emil struggled to keep his footing. Orange blasts blotted the dark horizon. The searchlights scored the skies without rhythm or rhyme; there were more aircraft than they could track. And no *Luftwaffe*. They had no air support at all.

The explosions tore through the streets, the fields without pause.

Then frenzy and wild-eyed panic.

"Firestorm!"

Just like Hamburg. Emil remembered the horror stories Georg had told him. The city of Nuremberg screamed— glowing flames enveloped the streets, entombing buildings.

Emil dove for cover.

Hot. So hot.

The heat sealed his eyes together. He couldn't see. He stayed down, ducking.

257

"Get up, Radle!" Albert was frantic. Emil managed to stand, forced his legs to obey his commands. Peeling open his eyes, he loaded the Flak gun, lit the fuse.

Again and again, they fired into the sky. Just hold on, Emil thought, it will be over soon.

Another explosion. *Too loud, too hot. They were hit!* The base roared with flames, a gigantic fire pit.

The earth gave way and Emil lost his footing, falling hard.

The bunkers exploded, snapping like popcorn.

Katharina's station was down.

"Katharina!"

The station was destroyed. Debris everywhere. Emil started running. *Limp, hop, limp hop.*

"Radle! Get back here!" It was Albert, but Emil ignored him. He hopped and strutted, throwing stones and debris aside. He had to get to Katharina. Albert could shoot him later if he wanted. *Please, Katharina, be okay. Please.*

Emil saw her under the debris. He started digging through burnt wood and ash.

"Katharina!" He pulled her out from underneath it, bit by bit. She was still breathing. Emil held her in his lap. Her eyes flickered.

Bombs exploded all around them.

"Katharina?"

"Emil," she said softly.

"You're going to be all right." Emil whimpered. *Be all right, please be all right.*

A small smile. "So are you." He read her lips "Promise me?"

"No! Stay with me."

"Promise me." Her breath was shallow and labored. "You will be okay."

He shook his head. *Not without you.*

"Please?"

"I promise," he said weakly.

She closed her eyes.

"Katharina!" Emil shook her. "Don't!" He could see her slipping away. "Katharina! Remember our dream! Please!"

"It's still your dream."

"It's not," he sobbed. "I don't have a dream without you."

"I'm sorry, Emil. I love you."

She relaxed in his arms. He pulled her tight. "No, Katharina, please."

A screeching cry tore from his throat. Scorching pain squeezed his heart, slashing through his body as if Hitler himself had dug his nails into his flesh and ripped off his skin.

Chapter Forty-Four

They buried the dead in long rows in a farmer's field. Despite incredible human loss, civilian and military; despite the fact that nearly every major city in Germany had practically been incinerated; despite the knowledge that the lines on the east, west, north and south were all squeezing in, a stranglehold on the throat of the German nation, still Hitler drove the people on. It seemed he would not stop until every city was destroyed and every last one of his "beloved" citizens was dead.

Emil fashioned a cross for the top of Katharina's grave. She was his hope for the future, his reason to hold on, to believe for a life after the war. Now he had nothing. The pain of his sadness was so heavy, it was almost unbearable. But he lived on.

Why was Katharina dead and not him? He should be the one buried here. She should be safely tucked away in Passau with Johann.

Poor Johann. This would kill him for sure.

As they drove through the streets of Nuremberg, it was hard to believe Germany would recover. Ninety percent of the city was annihilated after a mere one-hour Allied bombing blitz. Emil wondered why they bothered to clean it. It was a wasteland, and their efforts were useless. He just wanted to go home. He was tired and homesick and heartsick. And Günther had more bad news.

"They didn't tell you, Emil, but I found out. I watched and I listened and I found out."

"Found out what?"

"The night of the firestorm, Passau was hit, too."

"What!"

"They didn't want you to know, because of our morale being low already."

"How bad?"

"I don't know. I'm sorry."

Emil flopped onto his bed as his mind shut down. He couldn't process this news. Mom, Helmut, Johann, they had to be okay. He couldn't lose Katharina and them, too. He just couldn't. He would rather die, even if it meant killing himself to accomplish it.

On January 27 the Red Army liberated Poland and discovered Auschwitz. Death camps. Furnaces. Large rooms full of bones. An atrocity of the worst kind.

Georg Stramm had been right again. *For once, couldn't that idiot just be wrong?*

Emil wanted to dig a hole and bury himself in it. Germany would never again be able to hold her head high. It had all been a gigantic lie. Their pride. Their strength. Built on death. Built on lies.

He lived on automatic, no emotions. Winter broke and spring arrived on schedule. Leaves budded and flowers bloomed, like Katharina had never died.

Had he really once worn the Hitler Youth uniform so proudly? Had he really marched with confidence, like it was all a game?

Emil hadn't heard word from home. The roads were out; he knew that there was no way for the post to travel. It didn't mean they weren't alive, but it didn't mean they were.

Bombs had dropped on Germany like a bad case of the measles. The country was sick. Very sick.

Emil had been right. The Allies were after blood, now. There was no way they could ever win this war, and yet the Americans and British relentlessly dropped firebombs on Dresden, near the eastern border. For three days. It was the worse firestorm ever, hundreds of thousands of people burned to death, mostly refugees from the east.

The news on the street was that Hitler was hiding. Their esteemed and fearless leader was hiding out in his little bunker.

Berlin was next. There was no keeping the Soviets out, now. It seemed Hitler knew it. He killed himself so he wouldn't have to watch.

Coward.

There was nothing left to do now, but surrender.

The war was over.

Millions of people were dead. No city was left standing. Emil didn't know if he would find his family alive.

And he hadn't even flown a plane.

Chapter Forty-Five

They were ready for the Americans when they arrived. They came with a convoy of army trucks, guns ready, but they showed no resistance, their arms were straight in the air in surrender.

"I'm scared," Günther said.

"So am I," Emil answered. The Americans leaped out of their vehicles, rifles directed at them.

"Do you think they'll shoot us, Emil?" Günther whimpered.

"Shut up!" said Hans. "You're going to get us all shot!"

The leader of the American troop indicated to his men to lower their weapons.

"I am Sergeant Corporal Elliot Jones. Who is the leader here?"

Most of Emil's crowd didn't understand English. Would they shoot them if they didn't answer correctly?

"Reimer." The Sergeant waved over one of his soldiers.

"*Wer is der Leiter?*" Reimer said.

They waited for Albert Jäger to step forward. He didn't.

What a pig! Emil thought. *Where was all his brave macho talk now?*

Finally, they all turned to stare at him. An invisible spotlight. Sergeant Jones strolled right to him and stood

263

directly in front of his face. Emil would swear Albert was shaking.

"Are you the leader here?" Reimer said. *"Sind sie der Leiter?"*

"Ja."

"Direct your men into the trucks."

Albert ordered them to climb into the back of the American army trucks. Emil had nothing but his light jacket and a small satchel that contained a pair of socks, a comb and a letter from home, an old one from Katharina. They dumped the contents out onto the ground before returning it to him. They let him keep the letter.

They drove them to an old monastery that was set up to serve as a prisoner of war camp. One of the American soldiers set up a large sign, written in both English and German. It said:

"Give me five years and you will not recognize Germany again." Adolf Hitler.

It wasn't just their group. It was filled with German POWs, mostly young men like Emil and very old men with thin silver hair and gray, stubbly whiskers.

"Will they let us stay together?" Günther whispered.

"I hope so."

The one they called Reimer instructed Emil and Günther to follow him. He took them to the kitchen and told them to wash the dishes.

Emil and Günther did what they were told. Reimer stayed with them directing the work in the kitchen and even pitching in to help.

Eventually, they finished washing the stacks of dirty plates and Emil and Günther worked to polish the kitchen. They wouldn't stop until permitted to.

Reimer watched them, puffing on a cigarette. "They sure taught you boys how to work, I'll give them that much," he said in German.

Did he expect Emil to say thank you?

"You don't look old enough to be in the army," he said. "How old are you boys, anyways?"

Günther looked like a scared rabbit. Emil answered for him. "He's fourteen, I'm sixteen."

"Just kids," Reimer muttered. Maybe so, but Emil felt like an old man. Reimer took a last drag and dropped the cigarette, squashing it under his boot.

Emil and Günther looked at each other. *Should they clean it up?*

Reimer left the kitchen and Emil rushed to sweep the cigarette butt up and dispose of it.

It was camp life, but far easier than any camp Emil had ever been to. Reimer took a liking to him and Günther.

"Reimer is a German name," Emil said to him one day.

"So."

"But you're American?"

"Yes, but my parents immigrated to America from Germany. If they hadn't, I would have been here, fighting for Hitler." He looked at Emil oddly. "I could have been just like you."

The next day, Sergeant Jones ordered all of the prisoners to line up, twenty in a line, ten deep, with their hands up.

What now? Emil thought. *Surely, if they meant to do them harm, they already would have.*

One by one the American soldiers left the yard. It didn't strike Emil as strange until there were only two left. All the blood in Emil's arms had drained out long ago and they throbbed, but he didn't dare drop them. No one did.

Then, only one American soldier remained on guard. After a short time, he too, left.

All of the prisoners remained standing, arms raised with no one guarding them.

"What's going on, Emil?" Günther said.

"I don't know."

Eventually one of the older men dropped his hands. Nothing happened. No sniping from the towers. Then another dropped his hands, and another. Still nothing. They all dropped their hands, rubbing their arms viciously.

"We're alone!"someone shouted.

Emil couldn't believe it. *The Americans had left them?*

The German POW's raced to the entrance and sure enough; all the American army trucks were gone.

They were free to go.

"What should we do now?"Günther looked small and frightened. Emil wished he could offer him more than a shrug.

"I don't know," he said. "Go home I guess."

The men moved around, dazed, until the truth hit. Then it was almost hysteria. Everyone began rushing away before the Americans changed their minds and came back.

"You'll be okay," Emil said. "Just follow the others who are heading north toward Berlin. I'm going to go back to Passau."

Günther swallowed hard, and stared at his feet.

"Günther?" Emil waited until the boy looked him in the eyes. "It was great knowing you."

Günther offered his slender, bony hand. "It was great knowing you, too, Emil."

Chapter Forty-Six

He hadn't eaten anything since the day before the soldiers left the prisoners in the field. Emil grabbed at his stomach and kept walking. He thought of his parents and his brother, imagining them alive and waiting for him to arrive at their home in Passau. He could see them sitting around the kitchen table, four places set. A roast chicken with potatoes and carrots sat on a platter in the middle, with large glasses of milk for all of them. They were waiting for him to get home so they could celebrate.

It was this dream that pushed him forward day after day. Then he saw a pillar of smoke rising on the horizon. It could only mean one thing: a farm, which meant food.

Emil limped across the sloping field, brittle and dry from lack of rain and irrigation. He lost his footing twice, falling, grabbing at his leg, his mouth opening in a teeth-baring groan. The first time he beat the pain, pulling himself back onto his feet, hunger pushing him on. The second time he gave into the primal urge to scream and cry, until sleep threatened to take him again. The warm sun beat down, heavy, his mind lapsing into a drug like state.

Somewhere in his subconscious, he knew he couldn't stay there; if he did he would die. He pulled himself up again, shaky and quivering. Finally a house came into view. Out of breath, he slipped through the narrow opening of a stiff iron gate and knocked on the door.

A cup of milk wasn't much but it was more than he'd had in days. He was starting to lose count. Every day was the same. Dry fields on either side of a broken road. Only the weather changed, some days were warm and sunny, others saw spring rain. Despite his limp and the pain, Emil walked. Walking, walking, walking.

When it rained, he lay down on his back, his mouth open wide, his thirst demanding, but never satisfied, drop by drop. Every so often he'd pass another wanderer, and they'd ask each other for food and leave mutually disappointed. At times, Emil was fortunate to get a ride from a passing farmer and gifted with a small portion of food. It seemed no one had much left over to share with strangers.

Emil constantly thought of Katharina, longing for one last chance to hold her and kiss her. When the pain of that was too much to bear, he'd switch back to thoughts about his family. Wishing for them to be alive. Father and Mother. Helmut. *Just concentrate, one foot after the other.*

A black wave washed over him and his knees gave out. Emil collapsed on the side of the road, semi-conscious. *Maybe he would die here? On the side of the road, half-way home.* His death would come not from bombs or bullets, but from starvation. He didn't even know for sure if he was walking in the right direction anymore.

Sleep came unbidden.

Someone was shaking him. His bad shoulder complained and Emil heard himself groan.

"Boy? Are you all right? Boy?" It was a woman's voice.

Groggy, Emil assessed them. A housewife with a gray dress and sweater, low-heeled boots and her short hair pinned back off her face and a young girl, dressed similarly, about twelve.

They tried to help him stand but his legs were too weak. Somehow they managed to pile him into their wagon and pull him to their home in the next village.

Soon Emil sipped hot thin soup in a small kitchen, sitting across from his hosts with a blanket around his shoulders. He had already devoured a thick slice of unbuttered bread.

The woman introduced herself to Emil as Frau Kohn and her daughter, who had yet to speak a word, was called Inge. When Frau Kohn offered him a second bowl of soup, he nodded yes, and by then he was eating slowly enough to answer her questions.

"What is your name?"

"I am Emil Radle."

"And do you live around here?"

"No. I am from Passau."

"Passau? That is a long way from here."

"Yes." Emil finished the last of his soup, and pushed the bowl away. Inge picked it up and took it to the sink. "I am going the right way, though, aren't I?"

Frau Kohn nodded. She picked up the tea pot. "Tea?"

"Yes, thank you." She poured him a weak cup and he drank gratefully.

"Who is in Passau for you?"

Emil paused. "I left my mother and younger brother there. My father was fighting in the North German Army. We haven't heard from him."

Frau Kohn wiped crumbs off the counter top with a wet cloth. "Why are you so far away from home?"

Emil sipped his tea then set the cup down. "I was a flight student in Nuremberg. At the *Fliegerschule*. But, mostly I manned the Flak."

Frau Kohn paused, mid-wipe. "I see. That was very dangerous?"

"Yes."

She motioned at him with her chin. "Is that how you hurt your leg?"

Emil shook his head. "That happened in western Ukraine."

"On the front? You are so young!"

"Not young enough, it seems."

She rung the cloth out over the sink. "I am tiring you out with all these questions, forgive me. Let me show you where you can sleep."

With a mattress, a pillow and blanket, Emil felt like royalty. He fell into a deep sleep.

Inge woke him the next morning. "Emil? Would you like breakfast?"

Breakfast was a heady feast of scrambled eggs and coffee. Frau Kohn boasted of her five laying hens in the back yard coop. "We're far enough away from the cities," she said in way of explanation. "The soldiers didn't bother us too much."

"Where is Herr Kohn?" Emil asked.

Frau Kohn bit her lower lip. "He is... missing. We are hopeful that he will return to us soon."

Emil nodded.

She continued, "Inge and I were talking and we would like to give you something for your trip."

Besides a satchel full of bread, Emil couldn't guess what else to hope for. He was in for a big surprise.

They led him out to a back yard shed and Frau Kohn opened the door. Inge went in and backed out a bicycle. Emil could hardly believe his good fortune. It was old and rusty, but it was like a carriage to him. Anything would be better than walking.

"Are you sure?" he asked.

Frau Kohn and Inge nodded in unison.

"Thank you, thank you." Emil took the bike, his eyes traveling over the frame. He felt like giving Frau Kohn and Inge a big kiss, but restrained himself. Instead, he stretched out his hand to shake theirs, first Frau Kohn's and then shy Inge's. It truly seemed to make them happy to give him this amazing gift.

Emil said his good-byes and headed off in the direction of Passau. The sun shone brightly and he squinted his eyes against its glare, enjoying the gentle breeze that blew through his hair. He was full and rested and best of all—not walking!

Emil covered a lot of ground over the next week, until came upon an American Army camp. The American flag flapped in the air and his curiosity was aroused. He wondered if Reimer was there and stopped to stare.

The American soldier seemed to come out of thin air. Emil hadn't heard him approach. Suddenly, he was nose to nose with Emil, speaking rapid-fire English.

He poked at the patch on Emil's shoulder. On it was a propeller with the name of his flight school inscribed.

The soldier shouted to someone behind him, and Emil realized he'd made a serious error in judgment.

He didn't understand a lot of English, but he did know the word "Nazi." He decided it was a good time to leave and lifted his foot to press down on the pedal. The soldier jumped in front of him grabbing his bike by the handlebars.

The soldier spit out angry words while shoving the bike, and Emil lost his balance, falling to the ground. He kicked Emil's bad leg, and Emil cried out in pain.

Just then, another soldier appeared. He spoke sharply to the first soldier.

The angry soldier wound up to kick Emil again. He covered his face, but the second soldier held the first one back.

The angry soldier shook free from the second one and they argued. The nicer one must have been convincing. Instead of kicking Emil, the mean-spirited soldier snatched his bike out from underneath him and swung it against the flagpole.

When the men left, Emil stood up and brushed the dirt off his clothes and decided he didn't need to see Reimer.

Emil tested out his leg. It hurt, but not more than he was used to.

He picked up his bike and examined it. He shook his head, but gave it a try. He could still ride it, only now it was bent in the middle and it only drove in circles.

It was back to walking for him.

Chapter Forty-Seven

JULY 19, 1945

Sometimes Emil would get help and food from strangers; sometimes his hunger would drive him to eating dirt, but each passing day brought him closer to Passau.

An American soldier pulled up beside him in his army truck. "What are you doing?" he said in German.

"I'm walking to Passau to look for my family."

"Get in."

His German was very basic, but Emil got the point. He wasn't sure if he could trust the soldier, remembering clearly his encounter with the angry one who liked to kick.

The American noted his hesitation. He asked in German, "Is Passau your home?"

Emil nodded. "Yes."

"I'm going that way. I'll take you there."

Emil got in and was shocked when the soldier shared his sandwich.

"You must register with the American army when we get there," the soldier said, mouth half full.

Emil mumbled, "I understand."

Two hours later, six weeks after starting his walk from Nuremberg, Emil was dropped off in Passau.

American soldiers moved through the streets, much like in Nuremberg. They still wore weapons, but since all German artillery had been confiscated, they weren't threatened.

Emil limped down the center of his hometown and was lost. He meandered like a drunk, his clothes shredded and soiled; and he smelled like he'd just trekked two hundred kilometers through open sewer, rather than through the rubble of broken highway.

A store sign hung from one hinge, squeaking rhythmically in the wind. It looked familiar; the image, the words. He cocked his head and narrowed his eyes: Jäger's Shoe repair.

He was in the right town. What the bombs hadn't destroyed, five years of neglect had. An unexpected flood of memories filled his head: his childhood, or the small amount allowed him, shopping with Mother, running, playing games with Moritz and Johann in the park, going to church as a family. It was beautiful and safe then.

And of course, Katharina. A lump formed in this throat, and he squeezed his eyes shut to fight back tears. Lots of painfully beautiful memories of her.

He collected himself and kept walking. For a moment Emil couldn't remember, was he sixteen or seventeen? Did he just have a birthday? He didn't even know the date.

Emil knew his way home from the park, and the anticipation of reuniting with his family at last propelled him on. *How would he find them? Helmut would be twelve by now, or was it thirteen? Was he able to take care of Mother? Did Father make it home from Berlin?*

He knew the odds. It seemed that every family had lost someone. Some families lost everyone. Boom. Gone. No more family. But Emil held out hope. They could be an exception. He made the last turn onto his street, stumbling on the jagged cobblestones.

Maybe it was the enormous dry knot in his empty stomach, or dehydration, or simply exhaustion. His eyes blurred over, and Emil felt faint. They lived in a two-storey, stucco, row-house..

It was gone.

All that remained was a row of burned-out holes, debris, and a silhouette of brick chimneys, tall and erect like a line of over sized soldiers.

"Mother! Helmut!" With urgency, Emil dragged his bad leg to their house, stepping over broken brick and stone, half burned timbers, until he found the steps to the cellar. Soot and dust stirred like a small storm and he felt the filth land on his face.

"Mother! It's me, Emil!"

Emil stepped down into the blackness. The ash was slippery like oil, and he fell hard on his backside. He bumped down one step at a time. Dry, mold-filled air invaded his lungs and he broke out in a fit of coughing. Emil wiped his eyes, squinting as they adjusted to the dark little room. The potato bin was still there, but it was filled with ashes now. Nothing else. Emil hadn't realized he was holding his breath until he let it out all at once.

They should be here. This was their safe place.

But it wasn't safe enough. The cellar was empty.

Back on the street Emil looked for someone, anyone he recognized.

Then he spotted Frau Fellner, the old lady from across the street. In the maelstrom of war and bomb destruction, her side of the street had mysteriously been left intact. Her house still stood.

"Frau Fellner!"

"Emil?" Frau Fellner's eyebrows pushed together. "Emil Radle?"

"Yes, it's me." Emil thought she didn't know him because he had grown, but then he realized it was because he was blackened with soot and ash. He wiped his face and brushed off his clothes.

"Please," he held her arm. "Have you seen my mother and brother?"

She shook her head, no. "I'm sorry, Emil. I haven't seen them for a long time."

"Do you know if they are alive?"

Again she shook her head. "I don't know. Some people have gone north to look for food. Maybe they went, too." She shrugged her shoulders, and frowned. There was nothing else she could tell him.

Emil looked north, and his hopes withered away. He had come this far, so many weeks of walking, of dreaming. He was meant to find them today, but they were gone. And he didn't know where they were, or if they were alive.

It was a sunny day. It would've been beautiful in normal circumstances, Emil thought. He stood in the middle of the street in Passau, in front of his burnt out home, sun beating down on his head and he didn't know what to do. The Nazis no longer controlled him, and the Americans couldn't seem to be bothered. He wanted someone to tell him what to do.

Suddenly his knees gave out. He didn't know if he wasn't paying attention to his bad leg, or if it was just a combination of physical and emotional fatigue. He was on his knees, in the same manner as his mother when she prayed.

Emil heard a choking, gurgling sound and found that he was weeping. He wept for Germany. He wept for Katharina. He wept for himself because he was alone and hungry and didn't know what to do.

Since he was down anyway, it occurred to him that maybe he should try it. Try praying like Mother. So he did.

When he managed to get up, he took one step north and then stopped. For some reason he felt the need to turn around and go the other way.

After a short while Emil saw a cattle path that cut across a field. It didn't make sense to go off the main road, and yet he felt compelled.

He limped through the bushes, careful not to catch his foot on twigs or rocks jutting out until he heard the babbling of a stream. Then he saw someone fishing.

The thought of fish made his stomach growl, and he wondered if there was any generosity left in Passau. Perhaps that boy would share his lunch.

"*Hallo!*" Emil called out. He was a ways away, and the sound of the stream must have drowned out his voice. He continued to call out until he was only a few meters from the boy and when he turned around, Emil's heart leaped. His face broke into a massive grin.

"Helmut!"

"Emil?" Helmut dropped his pail, and ran to his brother, pulling him into an enormous bear hug. "Emil! You're alive!"

"And you're alive!" It was strange for Emil to hear laughter coming from his mouth. "Mother?" He had new hope, "Father?"

"Yes! They're both here!"

Helmut grabbed his bucket of fish and led Emil through the trees to an old hunter's shack.

"I found this shack while searching for food," Helmut told Emil. "Father came home a few days before the bombs, and we hid here. It's a good thing we didn't hide in the cellar..."

"I know," Emil said. "I was there."

They walked through dense bush into an opening where a cabin stood. A thin figure was tending a small garden. She turned to them and her expression went from shock to joy. "Peter!" she shouted, "Peter, it's Emil!" Mother ran to Emil and covered his filthy face with kisses.

Father appeared at the front door. His left arm was missing, but he walked to his son and held out his right hand. Emil limped to his father and grasped it.

"Young man," he said looking straight into Emil's eyes.

They were two soldiers. They both knew. They understood.

"It's so good to see you, Father."

His father pulled him into a tight, one-armed embrace. "It is so good to see you, son."

Epilogue

Those in Bavaria considered themselves very lucky to have been occupied by the Americans rather than the Soviets. They'd heard things, word got out, and it wasn't going well for their friends and family in the northeastern areas occupied by the Communists. It was an irony, really. Hitler had been so passionate about eliminating the communists, and now they ruled the former capital of Germany, his beloved Berlin.

Well, at least half of it, Emil thought. The Allies decided to split the city up. He didn't know how that was going to work, but again, he was just glad he was in Bavaria and not Berlin.

The Americans treated them rather well, considering they were POWs of sorts. They organized new governments and rebuilding initiatives, but they weren't soft by any means. They aggressively rounded up all war criminals, the most famous of which went to trial in Nuremberg. They arrested Tante Gerta.

Emil always knew there was something not quite right with her. The prison for women where she worked was actually a Nazi Concentration Camp. She'd administered the extermination of Jewish women, and women who posed some kind of "threat" against the state. She was sentenced to death for war crimes.

Everyone on their street worked together to rebuild the neighborhood. Even though Father only had one arm, he worked as hard as the rest. The first night they sat together around the table in their rebuilt home, Mother cried. She gave thanks for the meal, for the four of them being together again, and then they all said a resounding heart-felt Amen.

They missed having the Schwarzes next door. Frau Schwarz had been overcome with grief when Karl was killed. A short while later she'd taken her own life. The whole Schwarz family was lost because of the war.

Emil visited Johann regularly. Usually he was laying in bed, with the lights dimmed, his violin left neglected in the corner. Johann's mother was always happy to see Emil, and hoped that his visits would help draw Johann out of his melancholy. He took Katharina's death hard, as Emil knew he would. He told Johann over and over that Katharina would want them to keep living, and not to take the fact that they were still alive for granted. Emil said it to cheer Johann up, and eventually Emil started to believe it, too.

The Allies instigated a denazification plan. Anything that promoted Nazism was destroyed. Government policies were rewritten as was school curriculum.

None of the old teachers from Emil's school remained and they had no word of what happened to Herr Bauer or Herr Giesler.

The school building had been destroyed so now they met at the old Hitler Youth district office, in the same room where their unit used to meet. The room was much the same as before, except that the *Luftwaffe* model no longer hung from the ceiling.

It was a smaller space than they had at their old school, but they didn't really need a big one. Most of the kids were gone now, dead. Gone were Friedrich, Wolfgang, Rolf and, of course, Moritz. Anne was gone as were all the Jewish kids. Many others were gone too, like Katharina. Irmgard was busy raising a baby on her own.

In some ways it was like starting from scratch, Emil thought, like they were infants who knew nothing. As it was, Emil was too old to remain in school for long.

The adults in his neighborhood were called to an assembly to watch movies of the concentration camps and Emil attended with his parents. The Americans said they wanted to deprogram them. Most watched the films with disbelief, horrified. Some refused to believe it, all lies, they said. Still others burst into tears. Emil believed it all.

Eventually life became somewhat normal. The destroyed areas of Passau were rebuilt; the adults went to work and the kids went to school. They would never forget the war. The world wouldn't let them, and neither would history.

One afternoon Emil went to see Johann. As he walked up the road he heard the sweet music of Johann's violin. Johann was getting better it seemed. Emil listened closely recognizing the tune. It was a one he hadn't heard in a very long time, since before the war.

Emil smiled. It was one of Johann's favorite songs, *The Loreley,* composed by Heinrich Heine, a Jew.

The End

About the Author

Lee Strauss is the author of A Nursery Rhyme Suspense Series (Mystery Sci-fi Romantic Suspense), The Perception Series (young adult dystopian), The Minstrel Series (contemporary romance), and young adult historical fiction. She is the married mother of four grown children, three boys and a girl, and divides her time between British Columbia, Canada and Dresden, Germany. When she's not writing or reading she likes to cycle, hike and do yoga. She enjoys traveling (but not jet lag :0), soy lattes, red wine and dark chocolate.
She also writes younger YA fantasy as Elle Strauss.

Visit her at **leestraussbooks.com**

Author's Notes

It's never easy to write a war story. With World War Two being the most famous of wars, it's quite possible that I got some detail wrong, and a more studied reader will catch the error. That said, I spent countless hours researching and did my best to represent war time life as authentically as I could. If anything, reality was far worse than what was captured in these pages.

Though *Playing with Matches* is a work of fiction, I had the privilege of knowing a few people who were children during the war, and who shared their stories. I borrowed from some of their own true experiences to weave together some of Emil's fictional ones. Because of this, I consider this work a collaborative effort.

Acknowledgements

I owe a huge amount of gratitude to Emil Biech who shared his story of how he walked from Nuremberg to Passau as a teen at the end of the war. This became the seed that turned into *Playing with Matches*, and Emil Radle is named after him. The twisted bike story is his, as is the emotional impromptu prayer in the street that led him to the cattle path where he found his brother fishing in a creek. Emil Biech passed away on January 30, 2015 but a piece of his life will live on in these pages.

I also must thank my dear parents-in-law for telling their stories. The strafe incident belongs to Herbert Strauss and the potato bin that never emptied belongs to Martha Strauss. I also got the idea for Tante Gerta from a story about one of her grandmothers.

Inspiration and details for the train ride to the eastern front and some of the fighting sequences come from W. John Koch, whom I've never had the honor of meeting, but I'm very grateful that he wrote a book about his story. My gratitude also extends to Guy Sajer for writing The *Forgotten Soldier*. His account about his time fighting on the eastern front was invaluable.

A special thanks to Angelika Offenwanger for guiding me on German Culture, my Wattpad fan, Restintheshade, for army authenticity notes and to Claudia Dahinden for her hard work and insights on the German language translation.

And to all those people who dare to resist evil in any age—thank you.

Recommended Reading

No Escape: My Young Years Under Hitler's Shadow - by W. John Koch

Hitler Youth: Growing Up in Hitler's Shadow - by Susan Campbell Bartoletti

The White Rose: Munich, 1942-1943 by Inge Scholl, Arthur R. Schultz and Dorothee Soelle

When Truth Was Treason: German Youth against Hitler: The Story of the Helmuth Huebener Group, based on the Narrative of Karl Heinz Schnibbe by Blair R Holmes, Alan Keele and Karl Heinz Schnibbe

The Forgotten Soldier by Guy Sajer

Made in the USA
San Bernardino, CA
15 May 2017